The FIRST EGG HUNT

Adam & Charlotte Guillain

Pippa Curnick

EGMONT

"It's very nearly **Easter**,"
Bunny said to his friend, Chick.
They were working through their list
And checking jobs off with a tick.

DAYS 'TILL EASTER
1

EGGS OF THE WORLD
CHOCOLATE
LEMON CURD
Sprinkles
COOKIES

Chocolate Sauce
Sparkles
SUGAR
vanilla essence
Strawberry SAUCE

DARK CHOC SAUCE
Ribbons

Cocoa Powder
Chocolate Buttons
GLITTER
EGG DECORATION
candied orange
Chicken or Egg

EGG SPANNER
WOODEN SPOON

MIXING SPOON
EGG HAMMER
CHOCOLATE FUNNEL
TWISTY THING

SNACK
EGG CHISEL
EGG SAW
EGG WRENCH
EGG MAGNET
WHISK

BIG BRUSH

PLIERS

DRILL

SNORKEL
SPA
SMALL BRUSH

"Chocolate bunnies – **tick!**" said Chick.
"And chocolate eggs all packed."

"Our **best eggs** ever!" Bunny said.
"All neatly wrapped and stacked."

Then over moonlit fields
The Easter Bunny took his load,
And started his deliveries
With tiny Mouse and Toad.

Each beaver, bear and badger
Had a chocolate egg or treat.
Bunny made sure **every** creature
Would wake up to something sweet.

Chick gazed out of her window
And she clapped her wings with glee.
"We've worked so hard," she chirruped.
"I can't wait for them to see!"

Then, early in the morning,
Chick was woken by a cheer:
"Hurray for Easter Bunny!
He brings chocolate every year!"

The woodland creatures cried with joy,

"It's Bunny's best year yet!"

EASTER HQ

"But *I* did half the work," sniffed Chick.
"Did everyone forget?"

Soon fan mail started flooding in –

Now Bunny was a **star!**

They put him in a movie
And he bought a
shiny car!

BUNNY

Easter Bunny
Easter HQ
EAS T3R

Easter Bunny
Easter HQ
EAS T3R

Chick stomped away and grumbled,
"Why does **he** get all the fuss?
I'll hatch a plan to show their treats
Have come from **both** of us!"

A year passed, making eggs and
Checking jobs off with a **tick**,
But *this* time Chick popped labels
On each egg signed,

"Love from Chick."

"Chocolate bunnies – **tick!**" said Chick.
"And chocolate eggs all packed."
"Our **best eggs** ever!" Bunny said.
"All neatly wrapped and stacked."

"We're early," simpered crafty Chick –
And laid her cunning trap . . .
"Why don't you have a well-earned rest
And take a **little nap?**"

Then as the sun was setting,
While the Easter Bunny slept,
Chick filled the trolley up with eggs
And out the door she crept!

She trudged across the field with eggs
For tiny Mouse and Toad,

Then hauled her load up Badger's Hill . . . .

... But tripped up in the road!

"Oh, no!" Chick chirped in panic,
As the eggs rolled down the slope.

She chased the speeding trolley
And she tried to grab the rope.

Then, BANG!

The trolley hit a rock
And flew up in the air.

"Oh, goodness!" poor Chick whimpered

As the eggs fell . . .

Eggs landed in the bushes
And inside a hollow tree.

Chick panicked, **"I can't find them!**
It's too dark and I can't see!"

And when at last the sun rose
At the start of Easter Day,

The creatures
started waking up –

So Chick
just ran away.

Back home, the Easter Bunny stretched
And jumped out of his bed.
"Oh, no! I've overslept!" he cried,
Then frowned and scratched his head.

He saw the eggs had disappeared
And gave a little wail.

Just then a tearful Chick burst in
And told her sorry tale.

"I wanted them to notice me!
Oh, dear! What have I done?"

She closed her eyes and sobbed –
But then a voice called . . .

"This is fun!"

When Chick and Bunny crept outside
They saw the strangest sight.
The animals were rushing round
And squeaking in delight!

"I found one!" cried a little mole.
"Me, too!" exclaimed a frog.
A squirrel squealed and pulled an egg
From underneath a log.

When they saw the Easter Bunny
All the creatures gave a cheer:
"Hooray! We think your egg hunt
Is a **brilliant** idea!"

"My idea?" said Bunny.
"Things are not quite as they seem!
It was my friend, the Easter Chick –
We make a **perfect team!**"

"Three cheers for Chick!" he added
And they roared,

"Hip, hip,
hooray!"

Chick beamed and said,
"Let's have an egg hunt . . .

To Mary – CG & AG

To my amazing Mum,
who I love more than chocolate – PC

EGMONT
We bring stories to life

First published in Great Britain 2018 by Egmont UK Limited
The Yellow Building, 1 Nicholas Road, London W11 4AN

www.egmont.co.uk

Text copyright © Adam & Charlotte Guillain 2018
Illustrations copyright © Pippa Curnick 2018

The moral rights of the authors and illustrator have been asserted.

ISBN 978 1 4052 8628 2

SHAKE IT UP!

SHAKE IT UP!

Oona van den Berg and
Elizabeth Wolf-Cohen

ULTIMATE
EDITIONS

This edition published in the UK in 1997 by Ultimate Editions

This edition distributed in Canada by Book Express,
an imprint of Raincoast Books Distribution Limited.

© 1997 Anness Publishing Limited

Ultimate Editions is an imprint of
Anness Publishing Limited
Hermes House
88–89 Blackfriars Road
London SE1 8HA

ISBN 1 86035 298 7

Publisher: Joanna Lorenz
Senior Cookery Editor: Linda Fraser
Project Editor: Anne Hildyard
Designers: Alan Marshall and Eric Thompson
Photographers: Steve Baxter and Amanda Heywood
Stylist: Judy Williams

For all recipes, quantities are given in both metric and imperial
measures, and, where appropriate, measures are also given in standard
cups and spoons. Follow one set, but not a mixture, because they are
not interchangeable.

WARNING
A number of recipes in this book include raw egg. Eggs have been known to carry
Salmonella bacteria, which can cause severe and sometimes fatal poisoning. Use only
the freshest, best quality eggs and avoid using raw egg if you are very young, old or have
a compromised immune system.

Printed and bound in Hong Kong

1 3 5 7 9 10 8 6 4 2

CONTENTS

Fun Food & Canapes

A party is the perfect way to show off some of the prettiest and tastiest foods. And, because most of the preparation work can be done in advance, this kind of entertaining is generally much less demanding than formal dinner parties.

Planning the menu is the most enjoyable part of the preparations – informal or formal, large or small, close friends or business associates, the occasion will help you decide the right scale and approach. Time of day and the length of your guests' stay will also influence your arrangements – a few drinks with friends before going to a film will require only one or two nibbles, whereas a three-hour party after a family Christening will obviously need something rather more substantial.

Small pieces of food that can be eaten with one hand make the best party foods (remember that each guest will be holding a glass in one hand). Plan to have something to serve the moment people arrive, maybe a tray of crudités with a dip, as this gives guests something to focus on and helps them to relax. Move on to something hot when most people have arrived, then alternate between hot and cold, finishing with something warm or sweet. Serving sweet food is an ideal, subtle way of suggesting that the party is drawing to a close.

In this book, you will find easy recipes for simple roasted nuts and herbed olives, as well as more elaborate concoctions, such as wild rice pancakes with smoked salmon nests. But remember, with a little imagination almost any food can be adapted to a party-sized piece.

Condiments

Many different condiments can be used to put together a quick dip or snack at a moment's notice. Tomato ketchup and horseradish sauce can be stirred together with mayonnaise and a squeeze of lemon, to use as a dip for prawns or hard-boiled eggs. Or add chopped spring onion to soy sauce and mango chutney and spoon on to prawn crackers for another instant snack. The variations are endless – just use your imagination.

Barbecue sauce
Bottled barbecue sauces are ideal for adding an outdoor flavour to quick grills. They can be used to spread on pieces of meat or vegetables, then grilled and skewered onto a cocktail stick.

Capers
The little buds of the Mediterranean caper bush, preserved in vinegar, will add an extra piquancy to sauces and salads. They are especially good on pizzas and salads.

Chilli sauce
This bottled sauce is widely available in supermarkets and Chinese grocers. It gives a warm sweet-spicy tingle to most foods and sauces. Use in dips and marinades.

Dijon mustard
Indispensable for salad dressings, sauces and dips, as well as to spread on meats and cheeses. It is sometimes flavoured with green peppercorns or other aromatics.

English mustard
Sold ready-made or as powder to be mixed to a paste. This is the traditional relish for accompanying beef, ham and cheese.

Grainy mustard
The best known grainy mustard is from the region near Meaux, France, though English traditional whole-grain mustards are also available. It is delicious with ham and pâtés.

Horseradish sauce
This hot spicy sauce can be bought as a relish, or "creamed" which makes it slightly milder. Perfect with beef, smoked and oily fish, chicken and seafood.

Mango chutney
Delicious with cheese or ham, or stirred into chicken mayonnaise, egg mayonnaise or diced lamb.

Mayonnaise
A good-quality mayonnaise is indispensable. Use as a dip or a spread or to bind chopped hard-boiled eggs or chicken into toppings for toasts to serve as a quick canapé. Making your own is worth the effort.

Plum sauce
Made from plums, apricots, garlic, chillies, sugar, vinegar and flavourings, this thick, sweet Cantonese condiment makes an ideal dip for Chinese-style snacks, or base for a barbecue sauce.

Soy sauce
This sauce is the basis of many Chinese-style dips and sauces. (Light soy sauce is more common than dark, but it is more salty. Dilute it with a little water.) Add chopped spring onions and coriander for an easy dipping sauce.

Sweetcorn relish
This sweet and tangy relish for hamburgers can also be used to top slices of cold chicken, beef or ham or hard-boiled eggs.

Tartare sauce
This is the standard sauce for fried fish and seafood. It is delicious with fish cakes. A mixture of mayonnaise, sweet gherkins, spring onions, capers and vinegar; try making your own.

Tomato chutney
Chutneys of all kinds make a tasty accompaniment to cold meats and salamis as well as cheeses and cold grilled vegetables.

Tomato ketchup
This universal condiment can be used in barbecue sauces and marinades or spread on toast and top with cheese or meats for a quick canapé.

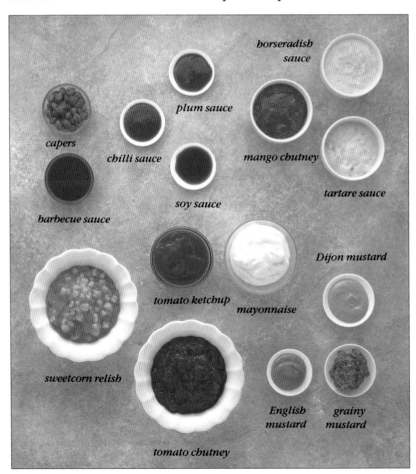

capers
barbecue sauce
chilli sauce
plum sauce
soy sauce
horseradish sauce
mango chutney
tartare sauce
sweetcorn relish
tomato ketchup
mayonnaise
tomato chutney
English mustard
grainy mustard
Dijon mustard

Herbs

Fresh herbs can be used generously in party foods, as they provide fresh flavour and interest to many different dishes. They also make a simple but elegant garnish. Use the same herb that you use in a recipe to garnish the serving plate – this provides a hint of what's in the food.

If you are lucky enough to have a garden, or even a window-box, grow your own herbs so you will always have some to hand. If you can't grow your own, choose from the extensive range of fresh herbs now available from supermarkets.

flat-leaf parsley

mint

lemon grass

watercress

bay

chives

dill

thyme

oregano

basil

coriander

Basil
The warm, spicy scent of basil epitomizes the flavours of the Mediterranean. Use it with tomatoes, summer salad, vegetable dishes and of course in pesto with pine nuts and Parmesan cheese.

Bay
This leaf of the laurel family gives a delicate flavour to soups, casseroles and pâtés. Bay leaves make a pretty garnish which will stay fresh for hours.

Chives
A member of the onion family, the mild flavour is wonderful with almost anything, but especially in herb butters, cheeses, cream sauces, egg dishes and of course with sour cream on jacket potatoes.

Coriander
This wonderfully aromatic herb is used in Mexican, Chinese, Indian, Greek, Turkish and North African cooking, to add subtle spiciness to dishes such as stir-fries, curries and hummus.

Dill
Most often used in fish dishes such as the Scandinavian *gravlax*, the slightly aniseed flavour of dill is also delicious with eggs, potatoes, chicken and cucumber and soft cheese recipes. Its soft fernlike leaves make a lovely garnish.

Flat-leaf parsley
Sometimes called Italian or Continental parsley, this variety has a slightly stronger flavour than curly parsley. It adds interest and colour to almost any savoury dish, especially vegetables and fish, and makes a beautiful garnish.

Lemon grass
The stem of this lemon-scented, broad-leaved grass is used in South East Asian dishes, especially those from Thailand. If you cannot find it, substitute a little freshly grated lemon zest.

Mint
This herb, with its many varieties, gives a fresh tingle to fish, goat's cheeses, salads and is wonderful in dips. It is used extensively in Middle Eastern cooking.

Oregano
Sometimes called wild majoram, it has a powerful flavour used in tomato sauces and with vegetable dishes of the Southern Mediterranean and Greece.

Thyme
This intensely aromatic herb is used in lamb or chicken dishes. It is also good in tomato sauces and vegetable dishes and is an integral part of a bouquet garni.

Watercress
Technically, this is a vegetable and a member of the mustard family. Its peppery flavour is particularly good in sandwiches or with egg and fish and it can be used as an attractive garnish.

Store Cupboard Nibbles

It is always a good idea to keep a variety of nuts and other nibbles in the cupboard. Often a few crisps, peanuts or olives are all you need to offer with drinks before going out or before a meal. Look in speciality shops and ethnic markets for unusual nibbles.

Bread sticks (grissini)
Stand these in a jug for an easy snack on their own or with something to dip into, or spread each with a little herb butter.

Bombay mix
Commercially prepared versions of this Indian snack are now widely available. A mixture of fried nuts, pulses and other nibbles flavoured with curry spices – perfect before an Indian meal.

Cheese straws
These cheese-flavoured twists of flaky pastry look pretty and make a tasty snack.

Dried apricots
Dried fruit makes an interesting alternative to the salty savoury nibble. Also, try dried peaches, dates, prunes, figs and banana chips for a healthy snack.

Dried cranberries
Dried cranberries are relatively new in the dried fruit selection of most supermarkets. They are good on their own or mixed with dried cherries.

Gherkins
Little sweet pickled gherkins are delicious as an appetizer as well as being low in calories.

Green olives
A wide variety of olives is available in supermarkets. For a party snack the stoned variety are the most convenient. Spanish olives are often stuffed with tiny pieces of red pimento, almonds or anchovies.

Honey roast cashews
These biscuity-flavoured nuts have a slightly sweet, honey coating.

Japanese rice crackers
These puffs of rice with peanuts inside or wrapped with dried seaweed make a sophisticated nibble and look very attractive.

Macadamia nuts
These nuts come from Hawaii and Australia and have a delicate sweetish flavour. They are expensive but delicious.

Pistachios
Always popular, but often expensive, these pretty green nuts are sold still in their shells. Don't forget to provide little dishes for the empty shells.

Pitta crisps
These triangles of pitta bread brushed with oil and sprinkled with herbs, and baked until crisp and golden, provide a crunchy snack.

Popcorn
Plain popcorn makes a healthy low-calorie snack. Tossed with butter or oil and salt, it is even more delicious, but more calorific. Various flavours of pre-popped corn can be found in most supermarkets.

Potato crisps
Universally popular, crisps come in a bewildering variety of flavours.

Prawn crackers
These commercially made pale puffs are crunchy and scented with prawn flavour. They are often served in Chinese or Thai restaurants.

Pretzel sticks
A delicious crunchy snack, these salty sticks are handy to keep as a stand-by, and easy to serve.

Tortilla chips
Triangles of fried corn, these little tortillas are ideal with a drink or cocktail like a margarita. They are also sold with chilli flavouring.

prawn crackers

Japanese rice crackers

popcorn

macadamia nuts

cheese straws

tortilla chips

pitta crisps

dried apricots

Bombay mix

gherkins

green olives

pistachios

dried cranberries

potato crisps

bread sticks (grissini)

pretzel sticks

honey roast cashews

Garnishes

Garnishes on party food need to last longer than those on a dinner plate, which are eaten immediately – so keep them simple. Green, yellow and red tend to bring out the colour in foods, so stick to what looks best.

LEMON/CUCUMBER TWISTS

1 With a canelle knife, remove strips of peel down the length of the lemon or cucumber. Slice thinly then make a slit from one edge to the centre of each slice.

2 Twist the sides in opposite directions to form a twist.

RADISH FANS

1 Using a sharp knife, cut lengthways slits, leaving the stem end intact.

2 Gently push the radish to one side, causing the slices to fan out.

CHILLI FLOWERS

1 Slit the chillies lengthways and gently scrape out any seeds. Cut lengthways into as many strips as possible, leaving the stem ends intact.

2 Drop the chillies into a bowl of iced water and refrigerate several hours until curled. (The iced water causes the strips to curl back.)

SPRING ONION POMPOMS

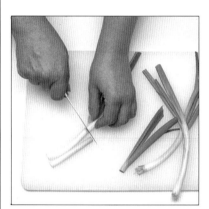

1 Trim the spring onions and cut each into lengths of about 7.5 cm/3 in.

2 Using a small knife, cut as many slits lengthways as possible, leaving the root end intact. Drop into a bowl of iced water and refrigerate for several hours or overnight until curled. (The iced water causes the strips to curl back.)

Cutting Carrot Julienne

It may seem a little time-consuming and fussy to cut vegetables into thin julienne strips, but the result is definitely worth it.

1 Peel a carrot and take a thin slice off each side to square it up. Cut into 2-inch lengths.

2 Cut each of the lengths into ¼ inch thick slices.

3 Stack the slices and cut these into fine matchsticks to form julienne.

Making a Radish Rose

This is a classic garnish. The technique can also be applied to the bulb of a salad onion or a baby turnip. Radish roses can be made in advance and kept in water in the fridge for up to three days.

1 Carefully trim both ends of the radish, removing the root and stalk.

2 Place base-end down and cut in half vertically, stopping the knife just before it reaches the base. Repeat until the radish looks as though it has been cut into eight equal segments, but is in fact held together at the base.

3 Put the radish in a bowl of ice water and let sit for at least 4 hours to open up.

Blanching

Blanching is a method of partial cooking, where foods are immersed in boiling water or boiled briefly. In terms of garnishing, the technique is used to make vegetables, fruit and herbs more pliable and easier to handle. It also helps to preserve a bright color.

1 Fill a large saucepan with water and bring to a boil. Add the prepared vegetable or fruit for the time suggested in each individual recipe: 1–2 minutes is usually ample.

2 Drain well in a strainer, then refresh in cold water. Change the water once or twice, as necessary, until the food is completely cold. Drain again.

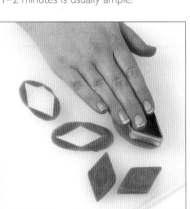

3 Blanched vegetables and fruit can be used in various ways: stamped out into diamonds, perhaps, or tied in a bundle with a wilted chive.

Peeling Tomatoes

It only takes a few moments to peel tomatoes, but the difference this makes to a dish is amazing. Concassing tomatoes (chopping them into neat squares) adds the finishing touch.

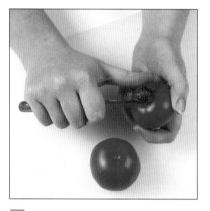

1 Make a small cross in the skin on the base of each tomato. Use a small sharp knife to cut out the calyx.

2 Place the tomatoes in boiling water for 20–30 seconds, drain and refresh under cold water. Gently peel off the loosened skin.

3 Cut the tomatoes into quarters. Place each tomato quarter flesh-side down and slide a knife along the inner flesh, scooping out all the seeds. Cut the flesh into neat ¼-inch squares.

Roasting Sweet Peppers

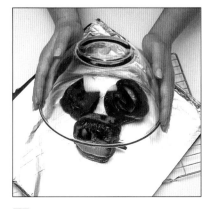

1 Place the peppers on a foil-lined baking sheet and grill until blackened and blistered on all sides, turning occasionally. Cover the peppers with a large bowl or place in a plastic bag and seal, until cool.

2 Using a sharp knife, peel off the charred skin. Cut the peppers into strips, removing the core and seeds but reserving any juices.

Lining Small Tartlet Tins

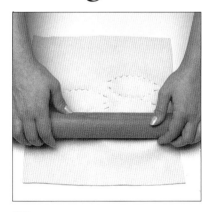

1 Roll out the dough as the recipe directs. Arrange the tartlet tins close to each other on a work surface. Roll the dough loosely back on to the rolling pin then roll out over the tins. Roll the rolling pin firmly over the dough to cut the edges.

2 Using both thumbs, carefully press the dough into the bottom and up the sides of the tins.

Using a Canelle Knife

1 Holding the fruit or vegetable in one hand, pull the canelle knife along the surface at regular intervals to create grooves in the surface.

2 Cut the fruit or vegetable horizontally to make pretty, ridged slices.

Easy Sauces and Spreads

MAYONNAISE

Home-made mayonnaise is well worth making to use as a spread or dip. If you like, add some herbs along with the egg yolks. Remember mayonnaise is made with raw egg yolks, so use fresh eggs from a good supplier. Raw eggs are not suitable for young children, the elderly or pregnant women.

Makes about 350 ml/12 fl oz/1½ cups

INGREDIENTS
2 egg yolks
15 ml/1 tbsp Dijon mustard
15 ml/1 tbsp white wine vinegar
300 ml/½ pint/1¼ cups olive oil or
 half olive oil and half sunflower oil

1 Put the egg yolks in the bowl of a food processor. Add the mustard and vinegar and process for 10 seconds to blend.

2 With the machine running, gradually pour the oil through the feed tube in a steady stream until all the oil is incorporated and the sauce is thickened. Add 15–30 ml/1–2 tbsp boiling water and process briefly to blend. Will keep in the fridge for up to 2 or 3 days.

EASY PESTO SAUCE

Pesto is a delicious sauce which can be used on its own or stirred into sour cream or mayonnaise to use as a quick dip. Use a good quality olive oil.

Makes about 300 ml/½ pint/1¼ cups

INGREDIENTS
50 g/2 oz/about 2 cups fresh basil
 leaves
1–2 garlic cloves
45 ml/3 tbsp freshly grated Parmesan
 cheese
45 ml/3 tbsp pine nuts, lightly toasted
salt
freshly ground black pepper
60–90 ml/4–6 tbsp virgin olive oil,
 plus extra for sealing

1 Put the basil leaves, garlic, Parmesan cheese and pine nuts in the bowl of a food processor. Season with salt and pepper and process until well blended, scraping down the side of the bowl once or twice.

2 With the machine running, gradually pour the oil through the feed tube until a smooth paste forms. Pour into a jar and spoon over a little more oil to seal the surface. Cover tightly and refrigerate, where it will keep for up to one week, or freeze in smaller quantities.

QUICK TAPENADE

Tapenade is an olive spread used in the Mediterranean as a tasty snack spread on toasts, or stirred into soups and stews. Keep it on hand for quick *crostini* or stir into soft cheese for an easy spread or dip.

Makes about 250 ml/8 fl oz/1 cup

INGREDIENTS
100 g/4 oz/⅔ cup Kalamata, or other
   oil-cured black olives, stoned
1–2 garlic cloves, chopped
15 ml/1 tbsp capers, rinsed

45 ml/3 tbsp virgin olive oil, plus
   extra for sealing
2–4 anchovy fillets, drained
juice of ½ lemon
5–10 ml/1–2 tsp chopped fresh

1 Put all the ingredients except the coriander into the bowl of a food processor and process until finely chopped, scraping down the side of the bowl once or twice.

2 Spoon into a small bowl and stir in the chopped coriander. Spoon over a little extra olive oil to seal. Cover and refrigerate up to two weeks.

BASIC TOMATO SAUCE

This sauce can be used as the base for pasta or vegetable sauces, as a pizza base or a seasoned dip. Use ripe tomatoes with lots of flavour and your favourite herbs.

Makes about 325 ml/11 fl oz/1⅓ cups

INGREDIENTS
30 ml/2 tbsp olive oil
1 large onion, chopped
1–2 garlic cloves, chopped
2.5 ml/½ tsp chopped fresh thyme
   leaves or 1.25 ml/¼ tsp dried
   thyme
1–2 bay leaves
6–8 ripe plum tomatoes
50 ml/2 fl oz/¼ cup water or stock
5–10 ml/1–2 tsp chopped fresh herbs

1 In a large frying pan or saucepan heat the olive oil over a medium heat. Add the onions and cook for 5–7 minutes, stirring frequently until softened. Add the garlic, thyme and bay leaves and cook for 1 minute longer. Stir in the tomatoes and water or stock. Bring to the boil and cook, uncovered, for 15–20 minutes over a medium heat until most of the liquid has evaporated and the sauce has thickened.

2 Pour into the bowl of a food processor and process until smooth. Strain through a sieve to remove any skin and pips, then stir in the herbs. Cool and refrigerate, keeps for up to four days.

Hot Pepper Pecans

These nuts are easy to make and can be prepared up to a week ahead, then stored in an airtight container.

Makes about 350 g/12 oz/3 cups

INGREDIENTS
15 g/½ oz/1 tbsp butter
15 ml/1 tbsp sesame oil
350 g/12 oz/3 cups pecan halves
15–30 ml/1–2 tbsp soy sauce
2–3 dashes hot pepper sauce, or
    to taste
15 ml/1 tbsp clear honey (optional)

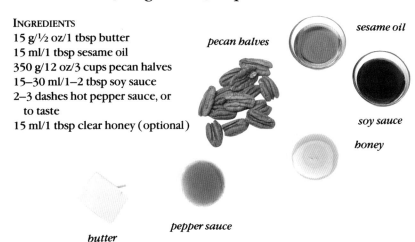

sesame oil
pecan halves
soy sauce
honey
pepper sauce
butter

1 Preheat the oven to 150°C/300°F/ Gas 2. Put the butter and oil on a medium-sized baking sheet and heat in the oven until the butter melts. Remove and swirl to blend. Stir in the pecans until well coated, then toast in the oven for 30 minutes stirring once or twice.

2 Sprinkle the soy sauce over the nuts, then add a few dashes of hot pepper sauce and the honey, if using. Toss the nuts until well coated, then allow to cool. Store in an airtight container.

Easy Nachos

This Tex-Mex speciality is popular throughout the USA, a spicy cheese snack that can be made in minutes.

Makes 24

INGREDIENTS
2–3 fresh or pickled jalapeño or other
    medium-hot chilli peppers
24 large tortilla chips
175 g/6 oz/scant 2 cups grated
    Cheddar cheese
2 spring onions, finely chopped
sour cream, to serve (optional)

chilli peppers
tortilla chips
sour cream
grated Cheddar cheese
spring onions

COOK'S TIP

When handling chillies, wear rubber gloves and be sure to wash your knife and cutting board well, as the chilli oils can irritate skin and eyes.

1 With a small sharp knife, split the chilli peppers and remove the seeds (the hottest part). Slice thinly.

2 Preheat the oven to 220°C/425°F/ Gas 7. Arrange the tortilla chips in a single layer on a large baking sheet lined with foil. Sprinkle a little grated cheese on to each tortilla chip and top with a slice of chilli and a few spring onions. Bake for about 5 minutes until golden and bubbling. Serve hot with sour cream, if you like.

Spicy Microwave Poppadums

This is a wonderfully easy way to prepare a spicy snack. Poppadums are traditionally fried, but this method is much lighter.

Makes 6 or 12

INGREDIENTS
6 poppadums, broken in half if you
    wish
vegetable oil, for brushing
cayenne pepper or chilli powder

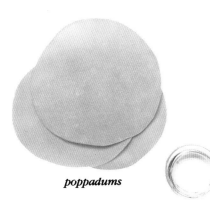

poppadums

vegetable oil

chilli powder

1 Lay the poppadums on a work surface and brush each one lightly with a little vegetable oil. Sprinkle with a pinch of cayenne pepper or chilli powder.

2 Arrange 2–4 poppadums (depending on the size of your microwave) on paper towels and microwave on High (100%) for 40–60 seconds. Serve immediately.

VARIATION

If you don't have a microwave you can make the same snack by using poppadums which can be grilled, and following the instructions on the packet after step one.

Hot and Spicy Popcorn

This is an ideal nibble for a crowd. Making your own popcorn is easy, but you can use the ready-made, shop-bought variety if you like. Adjust the chilli powder to suit your taste.

Makes 175 g/6 oz/12 cups

INGREDIENTS
120 ml/4 fl oz/½ cup vegetable oil,
    plus extra for popping
175 g/6 oz/1 cup unpopped popcorn
2–3 garlic cloves, crushed
5–10 ml/1–2 tsp chilli powder
    (according to taste)
pinch cayenne pepper
salt

vegetable oil

popcorn

garlic cloves

cayenne pepper

chilli powder

1 In a large heavy saucepan, heat the extra oil, then pop the corn according to the manufacturer's instructions.

2 In a small saucepan, combine the oil, the garlic cloves, chilli powder and cayenne pepper. Cook over low heat for about 5 minutes, stirring occasionally. Remove the garlic cloves with a slotted spoon, then pour the flavoured oil over the popcorn. Toss well to combine and season with salt to taste. Serve warm or at room temperature.

VARIATION

For Parmesan Popcorn omit the chilli powder and salt and proceed as above. After pouring over the seasoned oil, add 60–90 ml/4–6 tbsp freshly grated Parmesan cheese, and toss well.

Celery Sticks with Roquefort

This delicious filling can also be made with English Stilton or any other blue cheese. Diluted with a little milk or cream, it also makes a delicious dip.

Makes about 45

INGREDIENTS
7 ounces Roquefort or other blue
   cheese, softened
1¼ cups lowfat cream cheese
2 green onions, finely chopped
black pepper
1 to 2 tablespoons milk
1 celery head
chopped walnuts or hazelnuts, to
   garnish

green onions

*lowfat
cream cheese*

*Roquefort
cheese*

*chopped
walnuts*

celery

COOK'S TIP

For a more elegant presentation, fill a pastry bag fitted with a small star tip with the cheese mixture and carefully pipe mixture into the celery sticks. Press on the nuts.

1 With a fork, crumble the Roquefort in a bowl. Put in a food processor with the cream cheese, green onions, and black pepper. Process until smooth, scraping down the side of the bowl once or twice and gradually adding milk if the mixture seems too stiff.

2 If you like, peel the celery lightly to remove any heavy strings before cutting each stalk into 3- to 4-inch pieces. Using a small knife, fill each celery stick with a little cheese mixture and press on a few chopped nuts. Arrange on a serving plate and refrigerate until ready to serve.

Italian-style Marinated Artichokes

Good-quality extra-virgin olive oil together with fresh herbs, turn canned or frozen artichoke hearts into a delicious snack.

Makes about 750 ml/1¼ pints/3 cups

INGREDIENTS
2 × 14-ounce cans artichoke hearts
   in salt water
¾ cup extra-virgin olive oil
1 teaspoon chopped fresh thyme, or
   ½ teaspoon dried thyme
1 teaspoon chopped fresh oregano or
   marjoram, or ½ teaspoon dried
   oregano or marjoram
½ teaspoon fennel seeds, lightly
   crushed
1 to 2 garlic cloves, finely chopped
freshly ground black pepper
grated peel and juice of ½ lemon

thyme

*artichoke
hearts*

lemon

black pepper

oregano

lemon zest

*extra-virgin
olive oil*

fennel seeds

1 Rinse the artichokes, then drain them on paper towels. Cut any large ones in half lengthwise.

2 Put the artichokes in a large saucepan with the next six ingredients, stir to combine, then cook, covered, over very low heat for 8 to 10 minutes until the flavors infuse. Remove from the heat and leave to cool slightly, then gently stir in the lemon peel and juice. Refrigerate. Return to room temperature before serving on toothpicks.

Parma-Wrapped Grissini

This is an easy way to combine two well-loved ingredients for a quick nibble with no real cooking.

Makes about 24

INGREDIENTS
225 g/8 oz Parma ham, very thinly
   sliced
1 × 115 g/4 oz box grissini (Italian
   bread sticks)
basil leaves, to garnish (optional)

grissini

basil leaves

Parma ham

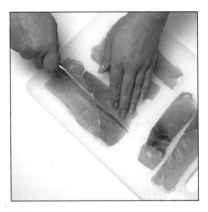

1 If the Parma ham slices are large, lay each slice flat on a board and cut in half lengthways.

2 Wrap each bread stick with a half-slice of Parma ham, tucking in a basil leaf if you like, to come half way down the bread stick. Arrange on a plate and cover until ready to serve. Garnish with fresh basil if you like.

COOK'S TIP

Do not prepare too far in advance as the moisture from the ham will cause the bread sticks to bend.

VARIATION

Substitute half-slices of thinly smoked salmon and garnish with sprigs of dill instead of basil.

Aromatic Greek Olives with Feta

Prepare lots of these and store them in the refrigerator for unexpected guests. They will keep for about a month in a tightly closed container, but remember to bring them to room temperature before serving.

Makes 450 g/1 lb/3 cups

INGREDIENTS
175 ml/6 fl oz/¾ cup virgin olive oil
15 ml/1 tbsp cumin seeds, lightly
   crushed
15 ml/1 tbsp coriander seeds, lightly
   crushed
15 ml/1 tbsp fennel seeds, lightly
   crushed
5 ml/1 tsp cardamom pods, crushed
2.5 ml/½ tsp crushed red pepper
   flakes
1.25 ml/¼ tsp ground cinnamon
4–6 garlic cloves, crushed
grated zest and juice of 1 lemon
450 g/1 lb/3 cups Kalamata or other
   oil-cured olives, drained

TO SERVE
225 g/8 oz feta cheese, cut into
   1 cm/½ in cubes
15–30 ml/1–2 tbsp virgin olive oil
freshly ground black pepper
15–30 ml/1–2 tbsp chopped fresh
   parsley or coriander

feta cheese   *Kalamata olives*
lemon   *olive oil*
lemon zest
coriander   *coriander seeds*
cardamom pods
garlic cloves   *red pepper flakes*   *cinnamon*
fennel seeds

1 In a medium-sized saucepan, combine the olive oil, spices and garlic. Cook over medium-low heat for 3–5 minutes until warm and fragrant, stirring occasionally.

COOK'S TIP

The seasoned feta cheese cubes make a delicious nibble on their own.

2 Remove the pan from the heat and stir in the lemon zest and juice, then add the olives, tossing until well combined. Set aside to cool. Transfer to an airtight container or jar to refrigerate.

3 Bring the olives to room temperature, and pour into a bowl. Put the feta cubes in another bowl, drizzle over the olive oil, season with black pepper, then sprinkle with chopped parsley or coriander. Serve the olives with the cheese cubes.

Parmesan Filo Triangles

You can whip up these light and crunchy triangles at the last minute using fresh or frozen sheets of filo pastry.

Makes about 24

INGREDIENTS
3 large sheets filo pastry
olive oil, for brushing
45–60 ml/3–4 tbsp freshly grated
   Parmesan cheese
2.5 ml/½ tsp crumbled dried thyme
   or sage

Parmesan cheese

olive oil

filo pastry

1 Preheat the oven to 180°C/350°F/ Gas 4. Line a large baking sheet with foil and brush lightly with oil. Lay one sheet of filo pastry on a work surface and brush lightly with a little olive oil. Sprinkle lightly with half the Parmesan and a little dried thyme or sage. Cover with a second sheet of filo, brush with a little more oil and sprinkle with the remaining cheese and thyme or sage. Top with the remaining sheets of filo and brush very lightly with a little more oil.

2 With a sharp knife, cut the filo pastry stack in half lengthways and then into squares. Cut each square into triangles.

3 Arrange the triangles on the baking sheet, scrunching them slightly. Do not allow them to touch. Bake for 6–8 minutes until crisp and golden. Cool slightly and serve immediately.

COOK'S TIP

These will keep in an airtight container for up to three days, but handle carefully as they are very fragile. Reheat in a moderate oven to crisp when you are ready to serve them.

Nutty Cheese Balls

These tasty morsels are perfect for nibbling with drinks.

Makes 32

INGREDIENTS
115 g/4 oz cream cheese
115 g/4 oz Roquefort cheese
115 g/4 oz/1 cup chopped walnuts
chopped fresh parsley, to coat
paprika, to coat
salt and freshly ground black pepper

1 Beat the two cheeses together until smooth using an electric beater.

2 Stir in the chopped walnuts and season with salt and pepper.

3 Shape into small balls (about a rounded teaspoonful each). Chill on a baking sheet until firm.

4 Roll half the balls in the chopped parsley and half in the paprika. Serve on cocktail sticks.

Salami and Olive Cheese Wedges

Use good quality salami for best results.

Makes 24

INGREDIENTS
225 g/8 oz cream cheese
5 ml/1 tsp paprika
2.5 ml/½ tsp English mustard powder
50 g/2 oz/2 tbsp stuffed green olives, chopped
225 g/8 oz sliced salami
sliced olives, to garnish

2 Spread the salami slices with the olive mixture and stack five slices on top of each other. Wrap in clear film and chill until firm. With a sharp knife, cut each stack into four wedges. Garnish with additional sliced olives and serve with a cocktail stick through each wedge, to hold the slices together.

1 Beat the cream cheese with the paprika and mustard and mix well. Stir in the chopped olives.

Cheese and Pesto Pasties

These pasties can be made ahead and frozen uncooked. Freeze them in a single layer and then transfer them to a freezer-proof container. To serve, arrange the pasties on baking trays, brush them with oil and bake from frozen for 5–10 minutes longer than the recommended time.

Serves 8

INGREDIENTS
225 g/8 oz frozen chopped spinach
30 ml/2 tbsp pine nuts
60 ml/4 tbsp pesto sauce
115 g/4 oz Gruyère cheese
50 g/2 oz/½ cup grated Parmesan cheese
2 × 275 g/10 oz packet of frozen filo pastry, thawed
30 ml/2 tbsp olive oil
salt and freshly ground black pepper

Parmesan

olive oil

spinach

pesto sauce

filo pastry

pine nuts

1 Preheat the oven to 190°C/375°F/Gas 5. Prepare the filling; put the frozen spinach into a pan, and heat gently to defrost, breaking it up as it defrosts. Increase the heat to drive off any excess moisture. Transfer to a bowl and cool.

2 Put the pine nuts into a frying-pan and stir over a very low heat until they are lightly toasted. Chop them and add them to the spinach, with the pesto and Gruyère and Parmesan cheeses. Season to taste.

3 Unwrap the filo pastry and cover it with clear film and a damp tea towel (to prevent it from drying out). Take one sheet at a time and cut it into 5 cm/2 in wide strips. Brush each strip with oil.

4 Put a teaspoon of filling on one end of each strip of pastry. Fold the end over in a triangle, enclosing the filling.

5 Continue to fold the triangle over and over again until the end of the strip is reached. Repeat with the other strips, until all the filling has been used up.

6 Place the pasties on baking trays, brush them with oil and bake for 20–25 minutes, or until golden brown. Cool on a wire rack. Serve warm.

Spiced Mixed Nuts

Spices are a delicious addition to mixed roasted nuts.

Makes 350 g/12 oz/2 cups

INGREDIENTS
115 g/4 oz/⅔ cup brazil nuts
115 g/4 oz/⅔ cup cashew nuts
115 g/4 oz/⅔ cup almonds
2.5 ml/½ tsp mild chilli powder
2.5 ml/½ tsp ground coriander
2.5 ml/½ tsp salt
25 g/1 oz/2 tbsp butter, melted

1 Preheat the oven to 180°C/350°F/ Gas 4. Put all the nuts and spices and the salt on to a baking tray and mix well.

2 Pour over the melted butter and bake for 10–15 minutes, stirring until golden brown.

3 Drain on kitchen paper and allow to cool before serving.

Herby Cheese Biscuits

Use a selection of festive shapes for cutting out these biscuits.

Makes 32

INGREDIENTS
350 g/12 oz/3 cups plain flour
2.5 ml/½ tsp cayenne pepper
5 ml/1 tsp English mustard powder
175 g/6 oz/¾ cup butter
175 g/6 oz strong Cheddar cheese, grated finely
15 ml/1 tbsp mixed dried herbs
1 egg, beaten
salt and freshly ground black pepper

2 Rub the butter into the flour and add the cheese, herbs and seasoning. Stir in the beaten egg to bind, and knead to a smooth dough.

1 Preheat the oven to 200°C/400°F/ Gas 6. Sift the flour, cayenne pepper and mustard powder together into a bowl or food processor.

3 On a lightly floured work surface, roll the dough out thinly. Stamp it into small biscuits with cutters. Bake for 10–15 minutes, or until golden. Cool on a wire rack. Store in an airtight container.

Mini Macaroons

Try these chewy macaroons with a glass of wine – in France, sweet biscuits are often served with Champagne.

Makes about 34

INGREDIENTS
150 g/5 oz/1¼ cups blanched
  almonds
150 g/5 oz/⅔ cup + 15 ml/1 tbsp
  caster sugar
2 egg whites
2.5 ml/½ tsp almond or natural vanilla
  essence
icing sugar, for dusting (optional)

egg white

caster sugar

almond
essence

blanched almonds

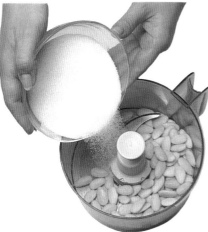

1 Preheat the oven to 200°C/400°F/ Gas 6. Line a large baking sheet with non-stick baking parchment. Put the almonds and sugar in the bowl of a food processor and process until very finely ground. With the machine running, slowly add the egg whites. (You may not need all of them; the dough should be soft but hold its shape.) If the mixture is too stiff, add a little more egg white. Carefully mix in the almond or vanilla essence.

2 With moistened hands, shape the mixture into about 34 small balls and arrange on the baking sheet about 4 cm/1½ in apart. With the back of a wet spoon, flatten the tops and dust lightly with icing sugar.

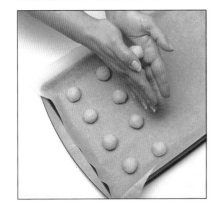

3 Bake for 12–15 minutes until the tops just begin to colour and the macaroons feel slightly firm. Transfer the baking sheet to a wire rack to cool, dust with more icing sugar if you like, then remove the macaroons from the paper.

VARIATION

If you like, press an extra blanched almond half on top of each macaroon before baking.

Crudités and Dips

Dips and their accompanying raw vegetables – crudités – seem to be an inevitable feature of any informal gathering, because they are such ideal party food. Just about anything can be included in the crudité category – asparagus spears, courgettes, raw or blanched vegetables, strips of cheese, melon, cooked chicken . . . all these can be dipped into a variety of mixtures that come from around the world – guacamole from Mexico, hummus and taramasalata from Greece, sweet mustard sauce from Sweden, spicy dhal from India, olivada from Spain or tapenade from France. The following two dips are easy to make and can be prepared at the last minute.

Slicing Peppers

1 Cut off the bottom of the pepper and stand the pepper on the cut edge. Cut down each side of the core to obtain 4 flat sides.

2 Cut each side into triangular-shaped spears to serve as crudités.

Easy Oriental Dip

Makes about 250 ml/ 8 fl oz/1 cup

INGREDIENTS
120 ml/4 fl oz/½ cup sunflower oil
50 ml/2 fl oz/¼ cup toasted sesame oil
2.5 cm/1 in piece fresh root ginger, peeled
1–2 garlic cloves, crushed
2 spring onions, finely chopped
1 small red chilli, seeds removed, finely chopped

spring onions

sesame oil

soy sauce

root ginger

garlic

sunflower oil

1 Heat the oils in a small saucepan over a low heat. Cut the peeled root ginger into thin slices. Stack the slices and cut into long thin julienne strips.

2 Turn the strips and cut crossways into very small dice. Put the diced ginger, garlic, spring onions and chilli into the oil and heat for 5–7 minutes, to allow the flavours to infuse. Cool and pour into a small bowl and serve with crudités.

VARIATION

Try making a sour cream and herb dip
by mixing together 250 ml/8 oz/1 cup
sour cream, 2 spring onions finely
chopped, and sprigs of fresh herbs
such as dill, parsley and chives.
Season with black pepper, you can
also add crushed garlic to this dip.

Slicing Fennel

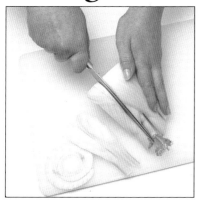

1 Trim the tops and root end of the
fennel bulb. If you like, remove the
triangular core and cut the bulb in
half lengthways.

2 Cut each half into long strips to serve
as crudités.

Tortelloni Kebabs

This hors d'oeuvres is easy to make, and always popular. Any favourite dipping sauce can be substituted, or just drizzle the kebabs with good virgin olive oil and sprinkle with freshly grated Parmesan.

Makes about 64

INGREDIENTS
450 g/1 lb fresh cheese-filled
    tortelloni
10 ml/2 tsp olive oil
basil leaves, to garnish

FOR THE SAUCE
1 × 450 g/16 oz jar roasted red
    peppers, drained
1 garlic clove, chopped
15 ml/1 tbsp olive oil
15 ml/1 tbsp balsamic vinegar
5 ml/1 tsp sugar
freshly ground black pepper
2–3 dashes hot pepper sauce

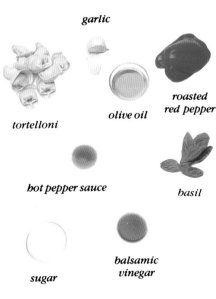

garlic

olive oil

roasted
red pepper

tortelloni

hot pepper sauce

basil

balsamic
vinegar

sugar

1 Put the ingredients for the sauce into the bowl of a food processor and process until smooth, scraping down the sides once or twice. Sieve into a serving bowl and cover until ready to serve.

2 Bring a large saucepan of lightly salted water to a fast boil. Add the tortelloni and cook according to the instructions on the packet, for 8–10 minutes. Drain, rinse in warm water and turn into a bowl. Toss with olive oil to prevent sticking. Cover until ready to serve.

3 Using small, 15 cm/6 in wooden skewers, thread a basil leaf and 1 tortelloni on to each skewer. Arrange on a plate and serve warm, or at room temperature with the dipping sauce.

COOK'S TIP

The sauce can be made up to a day in advance or frozen for several weeks.

Hot Salt Beef on a Stick

This quick nibble on a stick is based on the famous New York delicatessen sandwich, pastrami on rye.

Makes 24

INGREDIENTS
vegetable oil, for frying
unsliced rye bread with caraway
    seeds, cut into 24 1 cm/½ in cubes
225 g/8 oz salt beef or pastrami, in one
    piece
mild mustard, for spreading
2 pickled cucumbers, cut into
    small pieces
24 cocktail onions

salt beef

rye bread

mustard

cocktail onions

pickled cucumbers

1 In a heavy medium-sized frying pan, heat 1 cm/½ in of oil. When very hot but not smoking add half the bread cubes and fry for about 1 minute until just golden, turning occasionally. Remove with a slotted spoon and drain on a paper towel. Repeat with the remaining cubes.

2 Cut the salt beef or pastrami into 1 cm/½ in cubes and spread one side of each cube with a little mustard.

3 Thread a bread cube on to a skewer then a piece of meat with the mustard side against the bread, then a piece of pickled cucumber, and finally an onion. Arrange the skewers on a plate or tray, and serve immediately.

Medjoul Dates Stuffed with Cream Cheese

These soft, plump fresh dates make an ideal snack. They are now available in most large supermarkets.

Makes 24

INGREDIENTS
24 fresh medjoul dates
225 g/8 oz cream cheese, softened
zest and juice of ½ orange
15–30 ml/1–2 tbsp Amaretto liqueur
  (optional)
50 g/2 oz/½ cup toasted almonds,
  coarsely chopped

orange

tortelloni

cream cheese

medjoul dates

toasted almonds

1 With a small sharp knife, split each date lengthways and remove the stone. In a small bowl, beat the cream cheese with the orange zest and 30–45 ml/2–3 tbsp of the juice. Stir in the Amaretto if using.

2 Spoon the mixture into a small piping bag fitted with a medium star or plain nozzle. Pipe a line of filling into each date, then sprinkle with the nuts.

VARIATION

You can use small dates but they are stickier and more fiddly to prepare.

Hot Crab Dip

This delicious creamy dip with a golden almond crust is served hot, with raw vegetables or savoury biscuits.

Makes about 600 ml/1 pint/2½ cups

INGREDIENTS
225 g/8 oz cream cheese, at room
  temperature
30–45 ml/2–3 tbsp milk
15 ml/1 tbsp Cognac or vermouth
2 spring onions, finely chopped
5–10 ml/1–2 tsp Dijon mustard
salt
2–3 dashes hot pepper sauce
15 ml/1 tbsp chopped fresh dill or
  parsley
225 g/8 oz white crab meat, picked
  over
45–60 ml/3–4 tbsp flaked almonds

crab meat

spring onions

cream cheese

Dijon mustard

dill

flaked almonds

vermouth

hot pepper sauce

1 Preheat the oven to 190°C/375°F/ Gas 5. In a bowl, beat the cream cheese with all the other ingredients except the almonds.

2 Spoon the mixture into a small gratin or baking dish and sprinkle with the almonds. Bake for 12–15 minutes until the top is golden and the crab mixture hot and bubbling. Serve immediately with a selection of raw vegetables or savoury biscuits.

Mini Jacket Potatoes with Sour Cream and Chives

Jacket potatoes are always delicious, and the toppings can easily be varied – from caviar and smoked salmon to cheese and baked beans.

Makes 36

INGREDIENTS
36 potatoes, about 4 cm/1½ in
   in diameter, well scrubbed
250 ml/8 fl oz/1 cup thick sour cream
45–60 ml/3–4 tbsp snipped fresh
   chives
coarse salt, for sprinkling

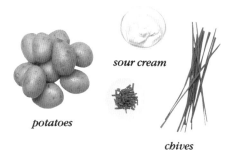

potatoes

sour cream

chives

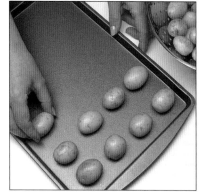

1 Preheat the oven to 180°C/350°F/ Gas 4. Place potatoes on a baking sheet and bake for 30–35 minutes, or until tender when pierced with the tip of a knife.

2 To serve, make a cross in the top of each potato and squeeze gently to open. Using the handle of a wooden spoon, make a hole in the centre of each potato. Fill each hole with a little sour cream, then sprinkle with the salt and the chives. Serve immediately, or at room temperature.

VARIATION

If your guests are likely to be hungry, use medium size potatoes. When cooked, cut in half, scoop out the flesh, mash with the other ingredients and spoon the mixture back into the skin. Serve warm.

COOK'S TIP

The potatoes can be baked in advance, then reheated in the microwave on High (100%) for 3–4 minutes.

Savoury Cheese Balls

These colourful little cheese balls are made in four different flavours, each variety coated with a different herb or seed.

Makes about 48

INGREDIENTS

450 g/1 lb/2⅔ cups cream cheese at room temperature
25 g/1 oz/¼ cup grated mature Cheddar cheese
2.5 ml/½ tsp dry mustard powder, prepared
5 ml/1 tsp mango chutney, chopped (optional)
cayenne pepper
salt
50 g/2 oz Roquefort or Stilton cheese
15 ml/1 tbsp finely chopped spring onions or snipped fresh chives
5–10 ml/1–2 tsp bottled pesto sauce
15 ml/1 tbsp chopped pine nuts
1–2 garlic cloves, finely chopped
30 ml/2 tbsp chopped mixed fresh herbs, such as parsley, tarragon, chives, dill or coriander

TO COAT

30 ml/2 tbsp paprika
30 ml/2 tbsp finely chopped fresh parsley
30 ml/2 tbsp toasted sesame seeds
coarsely ground black pepper mixed with poppy seeds

spring onions

Cheddar cheese

sesame seeds

garlic

parsley

cream cheese

poppy seeds

pesto sauce

Roquefort cheese

black pepper

dry mustard

cayenne pepper

chopped pine nuts

mango chutney

paprika

1 Divide the cream cheese equally among four small bowls. Into one mix the Cheddar cheese, mustard and mango chutney if using. Season with cayenne pepper and a little salt. Into the second bowl, mix the Roquefort or Stilton cheese and spring onions or chives and season with a little cayenne.

2 Mix the pesto sauce and pine nuts into the third bowl and season with a little cayenne. Mix the chopped garlic and mixed fresh herbs into the last bowl of cream cheese. Cover and refrigerate all four bowls for about 30 minutes, until the cheese is firm enough to handle. Roll each of the different cheese mixtures into small balls, keeping them separate.

3 Lightly dust the Cheddar flavoured balls with paprika, rolling to cover completely. Roll the pesto balls in chopped parsley and the Roquefort balls in sesame seeds. Roll the garlic-herb cheese balls in coarsely ground black pepper and poppy seeds. Arrange the balls on leaves, a plate or in a lined basket and serve with cocktail sticks.

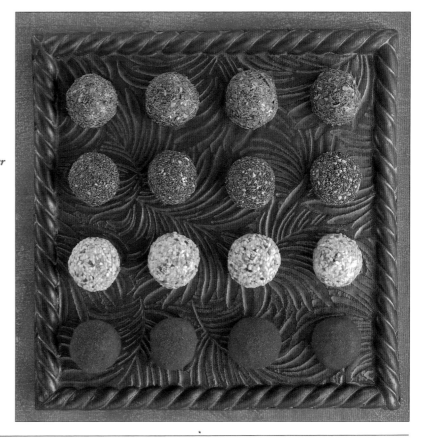

Crostini with Three Vegetable Toppings

This popular Italian hors d'oeuvre was originally a way of using up leftovers such as ham, cheese and pâté.

Makes 24

INGREDIENTS
1 ciabatta or French stick

FOR THE ONION AND BLACK OLIVE
  TOPPING
15 ml/1 tbsp olive oil
2 red onions, thinly sliced
5 ml/1 tsp sugar
2.5 ml/½ tsp dried thyme
16 Kalamata or other oil-cured black
  olives, stoned and halved
bottled tapenade, for spreading
  (optional)
parsley leaves, to garnish

FOR THE PEPPER AND ANCHOVY
  TOPPING
1 × 400 g/14 oz jar Italian roasted red
  peppers
50 g/2 oz can anchovy fillets
extra-virgin olive oil, for drizzling
15–30 ml/1–2 tbsp balsamic vinegar
1 garlic clove, peeled
30 ml/2 tbsp chopped fresh chives,
  oregano or sage, to garnish
15 ml/1 tbsp capers, to garnish

FOR THE MOZZARELLA AND TOMATO
  TOPPING
pesto sauce, for brushing
120 ml/4 fl oz/½ cup thick home-
  made or bottled tomato sauce or
  pizza topping
115 g/4 oz good quality mozzarella
  cheese, cut into 8 thin slices
2–3 ripe plum tomatoes, seeded and
  cut into strips
fresh basil leaves, to garnish

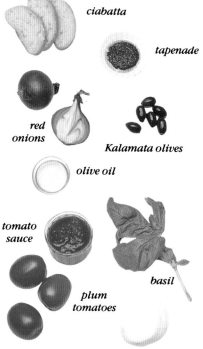

ciabatta

tapenade

red onions

Kalamata olives

olive oil

tomato sauce

basil

plum tomatoes

mozzarella cheese

anchovy fillets

balsamic vinegar

chives

capers

garlic

roasted red peppers

1 Cut the ciabatta or French bread into 24 slices, 1 cm/½ in thick. Toast until crisp and golden on both sides. Cool on a wire rack.

2 Prepare the Onion and Black Olive Topping, in a heavy medium frying pan. Heat the olive oil over medium heat and add the onions. Cook slowly for 7–10 minutes, stirring frequently until soft and just beginning to colour. Stir in the sugar, thyme and olives and remove from the heat to cool. Spread 8 of the toasts with a little tapenade and top with a generous spoonful of the onion mixture. Garnish with parsley.

3 For the Pepper and Anchovy Topping, drain the peppers and wipe dry. Cut into 1 cm/½ in strips and place in a shallow dish. Rinse and dry the anchovy fillets and add to the peppers. Drizzle with olive oil and sprinkle with the vinegar. Rub 8 toasts with the garlic clove. Arrange the peppers and anchovies on the toasts and sprinkle with herbs and capers. For the Mozzarella and Tomato Topping, brush the remaining 8 toasts with pesto sauce and spoon tomato sauce onto each. Arrange a slice of mozzarella cheese on each and cover with the tomato strips. Garnish with basil.

Grilled Brie with Walnuts

This unusual cheese snack looks impressive but requires almost no preparation.

Serves about 16–20

INGREDIENTS
15 g/½ oz/1 tbsp butter, at room
   temperature
5 ml/1 tsp Dijon mustard
675 g/1½ lb wheel of Brie or
   Camembert cheese
25 g/1 oz/¼ cup chopped walnuts
French stick, sliced and toasted,
   to serve

Dijon mustard

Brie wheel

walnuts

butter

1 Preheat the grill. In a small bowl, cream together the butter and mustard, and spread evenly over the surface of the cheese. Transfer to a flameproof serving plate and grill 4–6 inches from the heat, for 3–4 minutes until the top just begins to bubble.

2 Sprinkle the surface with the walnuts and grill for 2–3 minutes longer until the nuts are golden. Serve immediately with the French bread toasts. Allow your guests to help themselves as the whole brie makes an attractive centrepiece.

Spicy Oven-baked Potato Boats

These tasty spiced potato wedges are easy to make, and disappear so quickly it's a good idea to double the recipe!

Makes about 38 wedges

INGREDIENTS
4 medium-sized waxy potatoes, such
   as Desirée, scrubbed and unpeeled
1 garlic clove, crushed
15 ml/1 tbsp cumin seeds
2.5 ml/½ tsp ground coriander
2.5 ml/½ tsp ground black pepper
90 ml/3 fl oz/⅓ cup virgin olive oil
salt

garlic

coriander

potatoes

olive oil

black pepper

cumin seed

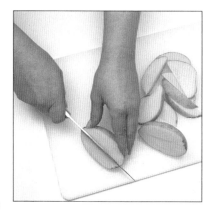

1 Preheat the oven to 200°C/400°F/ Gas 6. Cut the potatoes into boat-shaped wedges about 2 cm/¾ in thick. Place in a large bowl and sprinkle with the garlic, cumin seeds, coriander, black pepper and olive oil and toss to coat well.

2 Lightly grease a large baking sheet (preferably non-stick) and warm in the oven. Then arrange the potatoes on the baking sheet in a single layer. Bake for 30–35 minutes until tender and golden brown. Sprinkle with salt and serve hot.

Tiny Cheese Puffs

These bite-sized portions of choux pastry are the ideal accompaniment to a glass of wine.

Makes about 45

INGREDIENTS
115 g/4 oz/1 cup plain flour
2.5 ml/½ tsp salt
5 ml/1 tsp dry mustard powder
pinch of cayenne pepper
250 ml/8 fl oz/1 cup water
125 g/4 oz/½ cup butter, cut into
    pieces
4 eggs
75 g/3 oz Gruyère cheese, finely diced
1 tbsp chives, finely chopped

plain flour

eggs

butter

cayenne pepper

Gruyère cheese

mustard powder

1 Preheat the oven to 200°C/400°F/ Gas 6. Lightly grease 2 large baking sheets. Sift together the flour, salt, dry mustard and cayenne pepper.

2 In a medium-sized saucepan, bring the water and butter to the boil over medium-high heat. Remove from the heat and add the flour mixture all at once, beating with a wooden spoon until the dough forms a ball. Return to the heat and beat constantly for 1–2 minutes to dry out. Remove from the heat and cool for 3–5 minutes.

3 Beat 3 of the eggs in to the dough, one at a time, beating well after each addition. Beat the fourth egg in a small bowl and add a teaspoon at a time beating until the dough is smooth and shiny and falls slowly when dropped from a spoon. (You may not need the all the fourth egg; reserve any remaining egg for glazing.) Stir in the diced cheese and chives.

4 Using 2 teaspoons, drop small mounds of dough 5 cm/2 in apart on to the baking sheets. Beat the reserved egg with 15 ml/1 tbsp water and brush the tops with the glaze. Bake for 8 minutes, then reduce the oven temperature to 180°C/ 350°F/Gas 4 and bake for 7–8 minutes more, until puffed and golden. Remove to a wire rack to cool. Serve warm.

VARIATION

For Ham and Cheese Puffs, add 50 g/ 2 oz finely diced ham with the cheese. For Cheesy Herb Puffs, stir in 30 ml/ 2 tbsp chopped fresh herbs or spring onions with the cheese.

COOK'S TIP

The puffs can be prepared ahead and even frozen. Reheat in a hot oven for 5 minutes, until crisp, before serving.

Straw Potato Cakes with Caramelized Apple

These little potato cakes resemble *latkes*, a Central European speciality. You must work quickly, as the potato darkens very rapidly.

Makes about 16

INGREDIENTS
15 g/½ oz/1 tbsp butter
1–2 dessert apples, unpeeled cored and diced
5 ml/1 tsp lemon juice
10 ml/2 tsp sugar
pinch cinnamon
55 ml/2 oz/¼ cup thick sour cream

FOR THE POTATO CAKES
½ small onion, very finely chopped or grated
2 medium-sized baking potatoes
salt
freshly ground black pepper
oil, for frying
flat-leaf parsley, to garnish

potatoes

onion

lemon

dessert apples

sugar

cinnamon

oil

butter

black pepper

COOK'S TIP
Potato cakes can be prepared in advance and warmed in a preheated 200°C/400°F/Gas 6 oven for about 5–7 minutes, until heated through.

VARIATION
Omit the caramelized apple and top each cake with a few slices of smoked salmon, sprinkled with snipped chives.

1 In a medium-sized frying pan, melt the butter over medium heat. Add the diced apple and toss to coat. Sprinkle with the lemon juice, sugar and cinnamon and cook for 2–3 minutes, stirring frequently, until the apples are just tender and beginning to colour. Turn into a bowl.

2 Put the grated onion into a bowl. Using a hand or box grater, grate the potatoes on to a clean tea towel and squeeze the potato as dry as possible.

3 Shake into the bowl with the onion and season with the salt and pepper.

4 In a large heavy frying pan heat 1 cm/½ in oil, until hot but not smoking. Drop tablespoonfuls of the potato mixture into the oil in batches.

5 Flatten slightly and cook for 5–6 minutes. Drain on paper towels. Keep warm. To serve, top each potato cake with 5 ml/1 tsp caramelized apple and then a little sour cream on top. Garnish with flat-leaf parsley.

Angels and Devils on Horseback

The combination of bacon with scallops and chicken livers is surprisingly good. Prepare these in advance, then cook them at the last minute.

Makes 24

INGREDIENTS
12 rashers streaky bacon, rind
   removed
12 medium scallops, muscle
   extracted, rinsed and dried
salt and freshly ground black pepper
paprika
15–30 ml/1–2 tbsp chopped fresh
   parsley
12 small chicken livers, gristle and fat
   removed, dried on paper towels

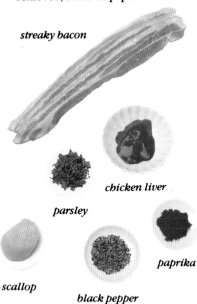

streaky bacon

chicken liver

parsley

scallop

paprika

black pepper

1 Preheat the oven to 230°C/450°F/ Gas 8. Line a large baking sheet with foil. Cut the bacon slices in half crossways and lay them on a work surface. Run the back of a large knife blade firmly along each rasher to flatten and stretch the bacon.

2 Place a scallop on each rasher and season with salt, pepper and paprika. Sprinkle with a little parsley. Place a chicken liver on the remaining rashers and season. Roll the scallops and livers up in the bacon and secure with a cocktail stick.

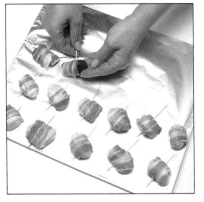

3 Arrange the bacon rolls on the baking sheet and cook for 8–10 minutes until the bacon is crisp and brown and the scallops and livers are just firm to the touch. Serve warm or at room temperature.

VARIATION
Fresh dates stuffed with almonds can be used instead of chicken livers.

Guacamole-filled Cherry Tomatoes

Cherry tomatoes are just the right size for an easy nibble; look for the yellow tomatoes in season. You can make the filling as mild or as spicy as you like.

Makes 24

INGREDIENTS
24 cherry tomatoes
salt
1 large ripe avocado, halved and stone removed
50 g/2 oz/⅓ cup cream cheese
3–4 dashes hot pepper sauce, or to taste
grated zest and juice of half a lime
15–30 ml/1–2 tbsp chopped fresh coriander

avocado

lime

pepper sauce

cream cheese

cherry tomatoes

coriander

1 Turn the tomatoes on to their sides on the chopping board. With a small sharp knife, cut a slice from the bottom of each tomato. Using the handle of a small spoon, scoop out the seeds and sprinkle the cavities with salt. Turn the tomatoes over and drain on paper towels for at least 30 minutes.

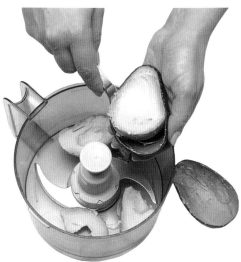

2 Scoop out the flesh of the avocado into the bowl of a food processor and add the cream cheese. Process until very smooth, scraping down the sides of the bowl once or twice. Season with salt, hot pepper sauce and the lime zest and juice. Add half the chopped coriander and process to blend.

COOK'S TIP
The tomatoes can be prepared the day before and stored, covered, in the refrigerator, ready for filling.

3 Spoon the mixture into a piping bag fitted with a medium star nozzle and pipe swirls into the tomatoes. Sprinkle with the remaining coriander.

Egg and Bacon on Fried Bread

These miniature "English breakfasts" are an amusing way to serve eggs and bacon as party food.

Makes 12

INGREDIENTS
olive or other vegetable oil, for frying
3–4 medium slices white bread
3 rashers streaky bacon, diced or
　　sliced
12 quail's eggs
cherry tomatoes, to garnish

streaky bacon

olive oil

quail's eggs

white bread

COOK'S TIP

The bread and bacon can be cooked in advance and kept warm or reheated in the oven when ready to serve, but the eggs should not be cooked more than 30 minutes before serving.

1 Preheat the oven to 150°C/300°F/ Gas 2. Heat about 1 cm/½ in oil in a heavy medium-sized frying pan. Use a 5 cm/2 in round pastry cutter, to cut 12 rounds from the bread slices.

4 Wipe out the pan and add 30 ml/ 2 tbsp fresh oil to the pan. Break in 4 of the quails' eggs and cook for 2–3 minutes until set. Carefully remove each egg and set on top of the bacon. Continue cooking the eggs in batches, adding a little more oil if necessary, until all are cooked and arranged on the bread rounds.

2 When the oil is hot, but not smoking, add the bread rounds and fry for 2–3 minutes until golden, turning once. Drain on paper towels. You may need to fry the bread in batches. Arrange the bread rounds on a baking sheet in a single layer.

5 Keep the eggs warm in the preheated oven until ready to serve. Cut the cherry tomatoes into quarters. Just before serving arrange the egg-topped bread on a serving dish and garnish each round with a cherry tomato quarter.

3 Pour off all but 15 ml/1 tbsp of oil and add the bacon pieces. Cook for 3–5 minutes, until crisp and golden. Drain well on paper towels, then put a few bacon pieces on each bread round.

VARIATION

If you prefer, instead of frying the eggs, hard boil them by cooking in boiling water for 2–3 minutes. Rinse under cold water and peel. Cut each egg in half and place on the bacon-topped fried bread. Garnish with a piece of chive or parsley leaf.

Herb-stuffed Mini Vegetables

These little hors d'oeuvres are ideal for making in advance and assembled and baked at the last minute.

Makes 30

INGREDIENTS
30 mini vegetables such as courgettes, patty pan squashes, large button mushrooms
fresh basil or parsley, to garnish

FOR THE STUFFING
30 ml/2 tbsp olive oil
1 onion, finely chopped
1 garlic clove, finely chopped
115 g/4 oz button mushrooms, finely chopped
1 courgette, finely chopped
1 red pepper, finely chopped
salt and freshly ground black pepper
65 g/2½ oz/⅓ cup orzo pasta or long grain rice
90 ml/6 tbsp/⅓ cup Italian passata (sieved tomatoes)
2.5 ml/½ tsp dried thyme
120 ml/4 fl oz/½ cup chicken stock
5–10 ml/1–2 tsp chopped fresh basil or parsley
50 g/2 oz mozzarella or fontina cheese, shredded

VARIATION
If you wish, after the first 10 minutes of baking remove from the oven, sprinkle the vegetables with grated parmesan, and grill for 3 minutes.

1 Prepare the stuffing, in a medium-sized frying pan or heavy saucepan. Heat the oil over medium heat. Add the onion and cook for 2–3 minutes until just tender. Stir in the garlic, mushrooms, courgette and red pepper. Season with salt and pepper and cook for 2–3 minutes until the vegetables begin to soften.

2 Stir in the pasta or rice and the passata, then add the thyme and stock and bring to the boil, stirring frequently. Reduce the heat and simmer for 10–12 minutes until all the liquid has evaporated and the mixture is thickened. Remove from the heat and cool slightly. Stir in the basil or parsley and cheese and set aside.

3 Prepare the vegetables, drop the courgettes and patty pan squashes into a large pot of boiling water and cook for 3 minutes. Drain and refresh under cold running water. Trim a thin slice from the length of the courgettes and the bottoms of the squashes so they sit firmly on the plate. Trim 5 mm/¼ in off the tops and scoop out the centres with a small spoon or melon baller; try not to make any holes in the bottom.

4 Remove the stems from the centre of the mushrooms. If you like, the mushrooms can be blanched like the courgettes or tossed with oil and baked in the oven for 10 minutes at 180°C/350°F/Gas 4. Allow to cool before stuffing.

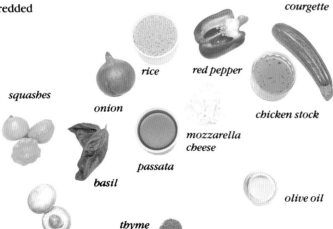

courgette
rice
red pepper
chicken stock
squashes
onion
mozzarella cheese
passata
basil
olive oil
thyme
button mushrooms

5 Preheat the oven to 180°C/350°F/ Gas 4. Using a teaspoon carefully fill the prepared vegetables with stuffing. Arrange the vegetables in 2 large baking dishes. Pour in enough boiling water just to cover the bottom and prevent the vegetables from sticking.

6 Cover the dishes tightly with foil and bake for 10 minutes. Uncover and bake for about 5 minutes longer, until the filling is hot and bubbling. Remove from the dish to a wire rack or paper towel-lined baking sheet if any water remains. Cool slightly, garnish with basil or parsley and serve warm or at room temperature.

Corn Muffins with Ham

These delicious little muffins are simple to make. If you like, serve them unfilled with a pot of herb butter.

Makes 24

INGREDIENTS

60 g/2 oz/scant ½ cup yellow cornmeal
70 g/2½ oz/⅔ cup plain flour
30 ml/2 tbsp sugar
7.5 ml/1½ tsp baking powder
2.5 ml/½ tsp salt
60 g/2 oz/4 tbsp butter, melted
120 ml/4 fl oz/½ cup whipping cream
1 egg, beaten
1–2 jalapeño or other medium-hot chillies, seeded and finely chopped (optional)
pinch cayenne pepper
butter, for spreading
grainy mustard or mustard with honey, for spreading
60 g/2 oz oak-smoked ham

whipping cream
plain flour
sugar
grainy mustard
ham
cornmeal
cayenne pepper
egg
baking powder
jalapeño chillies
butter

COOK'S TIP

Muffins can be made in advance and stored in air-tight containers. Bring to room temperature or warm slightly before filling and serving.

1 Preheat the oven to 200°C/400°F/Gas 6 and lightly grease a mini muffin pan with 24 4 cm/1½ in cups. In a large bowl combine the cornmeal, flour, sugar, baking powder and salt. In another bowl, whisk together the melted butter, cream, beaten egg, chopped chillies, if using, and the cayenne pepper.

2 Make a well in the cornmeal mixture, pour in the egg mixture and gently stir into the dry ingredients just enough to blend (do not over-beat – the batter does not have to be smooth).

3 Drop 15 ml/1 tbsp batter into each muffin cup and bake for 12–15 minutes, until golden and just firm to the touch. Remove the tray to a wire rack to cool slightly, then turn out the muffins on to the rack, and leave to cool completely.

4 With a sharp knife, split the muffins and spread each bottom half with a little butter and mustard. Cut out small rounds of ham with a round pastry cutter or cut into small squares, and place on the buttered muffins. Sandwich together each muffin with its top and serve.

Feta, Pimiento and Pine Nut Pizzettes

Delight your guests with these tempting pizzas. Substitute goat's cheese for the feta if you prefer.

Makes 10–12

INGREDIENTS
1 packet pizza dough mix
15 ml/1 tbsp snipped fresh chives
15 ml/1 tbsp olive oil
75-115 g/3-4 oz smoked salmon, cut
  into strips
60 ml/4 tbsp crème fraîche
30 ml/2 tbsp black lumpfish roe
chives, to garnish

pimiento

thyme

feta cheese

tapenade

pine nuts

1 Preheat the oven to 220°C/425°F/Gas 7. Prepare the dough as directed on the packet. Divide the dough into 24 pieces, roll out on a floured surface to ovals about 3 mm/⅛ in thick. Place on greased baking sheets and brush with 30 ml/2 tbsp of the oil.

2 Prick each oval with a fork, spread with a thin layer of black olive tapenade and crumble over the feta.

3 Cut the pimiento into thin strips and pile on top.

4 Sprinkle each one with thyme and pine nuts. Drizzle over the remaining oil and grind over plenty of black pepper. Bake for 10–15 minutes until crisp and golden. Garnish with thyme sprigs and serve immediately.

Smoked Salmon Pizzettes

Mini pizzas topped with smoked salmon, crème fraîche and lumpfish roe make an extra special party canapé.

Makes 10–12

INGREDIENTS
1 packet pizza dough mix
15 ml/1 tbsp snipped fresh chives
15 ml/1 tbsp olive oil
75-115 g/3-4 oz smoked salmon, cut
    into strips
60 ml/4 tbsp crème fraîche
30 ml/2 tbsp black lumpfish roe
chives, to garnish

crème fraîche

olive oil

smoked salmon

chives

black lumpfish roe

1 Preheat the oven to 200°C/400°F/ Gas 6. Knead the dough gently, adding the chives until evenly mixed.

2 Roll out the dough on a lightly floured surface to about 3 mm/⅛ in thick. Using a 7.5 cm/3 in plain round cutter stamp out 10–12 circles.

3 Place the bases well apart on two greased baking sheets, prick all over with a fork, then brush with the oil. Bake for 10–15 minutes until crisp and golden.

4 Arrange the smoked salmon on top, then spoon on the crème fraîche. Spoon a tiny amount of lumpfish roe in the centre and garnish with chives. Serve immediately.

Buffalo-style Chicken Wings

This fiery-hot fried chicken recipe is said to have originated in the town of Buffalo, New York, but is now popular throughout the USA. Serve it with traditional Blue-cheese Dip and celery sticks.

Makes 48

INGREDIENTS
24 plump chicken wings, tips
    removed
vegetable oil, for frying
salt
75 g/3 oz butter
50 ml/2 oz/¼ cup hot pepper sauce,
    or to taste
15 ml/1 tbsp white or cider vinegar

FOR THE BLUE-CHEESE DIP
115 g/4 oz blue cheese, such as
    Danish blue
120ml/4 fl oz/½ cup mayonnaise
120 ml/4 fl oz/½ cup sour cream
2–3 spring onions, finely chopped
1 garlic clove, finely chopped
15 ml/1 tbsp white or cider vinegar
celery sticks, to serve

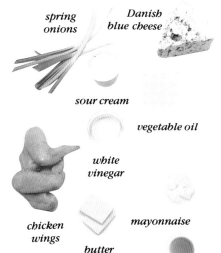

spring onions

Danish blue cheese

sour cream

vegetable oil

white vinegar

chicken wings

butter

mayonnaise

hot pepper sauce

1 To make the dip, use a fork to gently mash the blue cheese against the side of a bowl. Add the mayonnaise, sour cream, spring onions, garlic and vinegar and stir together until well blended. Refrigerate until ready to serve.

2 Using kitchen scissors or a sharp knife, cut each wing in half at the joint to make 48 pieces in all.

3 In a large saucepan or wok, heat 5 cm/2 in of oil until hot but not smoking. Fry the chicken wing pieces in small batches for 8–10 minutes until crisp and golden, turning once. Drain on paper towels. Season and arrange in a bowl.

4 In a small saucepan over medium-low heat, melt the butter. Stir in the hot-pepper sauce and vinegar and immediately pour over the chicken, tossing to combine. Serve hot with the blue-cheese dip and celery sticks.

Spicy Sun-dried Tomato Pizza Wedges

These spicy pizza wedges can be made with or without the pepperoni or sausage.

Makes 32

INGREDIENTS
45–60 ml/3–4 tbsp olive oil
2 onions, thinly sliced
2 garlic cloves, chopped
225 g/8 oz mushrooms, sliced
225 g/8 oz canned chopped tomatoes
225 g/8 oz pepperoni or cooked
    Italian-style spicy sausage, chopped
5 ml/1 tsp chilli flakes
5 ml/1 tsp dried oregano
125 g/4 oz sun-dried tomatoes,
    packed in oil, drained and sliced
450 g/1 lb bottled marinated
    artichoke hearts, well drained and
    cut into quarters
225 g/8 oz mozzarella cheese,
    shredded
60 ml/4 tbsp freshly grated Parmesan
    cheese
fresh basil leaves, to garnish
stoned black olives, to garnish

FOR THE DOUGH
1 packet pizza-dough mix
cornmeal, for dusting
virgin olive oil, for brushing and
    drizzling

2 Prepare the sauce. In a large deep frying pan, heat the oil over medium-high heat. Add the onions and cook for 3–5 minutes until softened. Add the garlic and mushrooms and cook for 3–4 minutes more until the mushrooms begin to colour.

3 Stir in the chopped tomatoes, pepperoni or sausage, chilli flakes and oregano and simmer for 20–30 minutes, stirring frequently, until the sauce is thickened and reduced. Stir in the sun-dried tomatoes and set aside to cool slightly.

1 Prepare the pizza dough according to the package directions. Set aside to rise.

onion
cornmeal
mushrooms
artichoke hearts
sun-dried tomatoes
grated Parmesan
virgin olive oil
basil
chilli flakes
pepperoni
black olives
oregano
mozzarella cheese

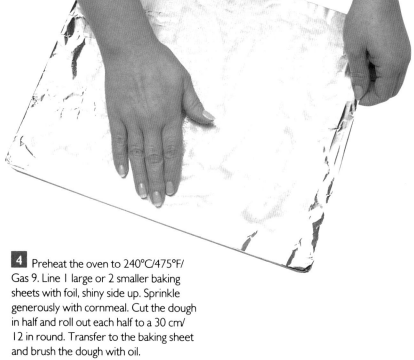

4 Preheat the oven to 240°C/475°F/ Gas 9. Line 1 large or 2 smaller baking sheets with foil, shiny side up. Sprinkle generously with cornmeal. Cut the dough in half and roll out each half to a 30 cm/ 12 in round. Transfer to the baking sheet and brush the dough with oil.

5 Divide the spicy tomato sauce between the dough rounds, spreading to within 1 cm/½ in of the edge. Bake for 5 minutes on the lowest shelf of the oven. Arrange half the artichoke hearts over each, sprinkle evenly with the mozzarella and a little Parmesan. Bake each one in the oven on the bottom shelf for 12–15 minutes longer, until the edge of the crust is crisp and brown and the topping is golden and bubbling. Remove to a wire rack to cool slightly.

6 Slide the pizzas on to a cutting board and cut each into 16 thin wedges. Garnish each wedge with a black olive and basil leaf and serve immediately.

Tortilla Squares

The Spanish tortilla is like the Italian frittata – a flat, baked omelette. Plain or filled, it is always popular.

Makes about 60 squares

INGREDIENTS

60–90 ml/4–6 tbsp olive oil, plus
   extra for brushing
1 large onion, thinly sliced
350 g/12 oz baking potatoes, thinly
   sliced
2 garlic cloves, finely chopped
2.5 ml/½ tsp dried thyme
salt and freshly ground black pepper
8 eggs
5–10 ml/1–2 tsp dried oregano or
   basil
1.25 ml/¼ tsp cayenne pepper or hot
   pepper sauce, to taste
165 g/5½ oz/1 cup frozen peas,
   thawed and drained
45–60 ml/2–3 tbsp freshly grated
   Parmesan cheese
red pepper, to garnish

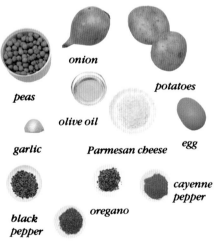

peas

onion

olive oil

potatoes

garlic

Parmesan cheese

egg

black
pepper

oregano

cayenne
pepper

thyme

COOK'S TIP

If you like, serve a small bowl of chilli sauce to use as a dip for the tortilla squares.

1 In a large deep, preferably non-stick, frying pan, heat 60 ml/4 tbsp of the oil over a medium heat. Add the onions and potatoes and cook for 8–10 minutes, stirring frequently, until just tender. Add the garlic, thyme, salt and pepper and cook for 2 minutes longer. Remove from the heat and cool slightly.

2 Preheat the oven to 150°C/300°F/ Gas 2. Lightly brush a 20 × 30 cm/ 8 × 12 in square or 25 cm/10 in round baking dish with 30 ml/2 tbsp oil. In a mixing bowl, beat the eggs with the oregano or basil, salt and cayenne pepper until well mixed. Stir in the peas.

3 Spread the cooled potato mixture evenly into the baking dish and carefully pour over the beaten egg and pea mixture. Bake the tortilla for about 40 minutes until just set. Sprinkle with the cheese and bake for another 5 minutes. Remove to a wire rack and cool.

4 Carefully cut the tortilla into 60 small squares. Serve warm or at room temperature with cocktail sticks, and garnished with pieces of red pepper.

Monti Cristo Triangles

These opulent little sandwiches are stuffed with ham, cheese and turkey, dipped in egg, then fried in butter and oil. They are rich and very filling.

Makes 64

INGREDIENTS
16 slices firm-textured thin-sliced
  white bread
120 g/4 oz/½ cup butter, softened
8 slices oak-smoked ham
45–60 ml/3–4 tbsp grainy mustard
8 slices Gruyère or Emmenthal cheese
45–60 ml/3–4 tbsp mayonnaise
8 slices turkey or chicken breast
4–5 eggs
60 ml/2 fl oz/¼ cup milk
salt and white pepper
5 ml/1 tsp Dijon mustard
vegetable oil, for frying
butter, for frying
pimento-stuffed green olives, to
  garnish
parsley leaves, to garnish

oak-smoked ham

turkey breast *white bread*

butter *grainy mustard* *egg*

Dijon mustard

stuffed olives

Emmenthal cheese

COOK'S TIP

These sandwiches can be prepared ahead and reheated in a preheated oven at 200°C/400°F/Gas 6 for about 6–8 minutes.

1 Arrange 8 of the bread slices on a work surface and spread with half the softened butter. Lay 1 slice of ham on each slice of bread and spread with a little grainy mustard. Cover with a slice of cheese and spread with a little mayonnaise, then cover with a slice of turkey or chicken breast. Butter the remaining bread slices and use to complete the sandwiches. Cut off the crusts, trimming to an even square.

2 In a large shallow baking dish, beat the eggs, milk, salt and pepper and Dijon mustard until well combined. Soak the sandwiches in the egg mixture on both sides until the egg has been absorbed.

3 Heat about 1 cm/½ in of oil and melted butter in a large heavy frying pan, until hot but not smoking. Gently fry the sandwiches in batches for 4–5 minutes until crisp and golden, turning once. Add more oil and butter as necessary. Drain on paper towels.

4 Transfer the sandwiches to a cutting board and cut each into 4 triangles, then cut each in half again to make 64 triangles. Thread a parsley leaf and olive on to a cocktail stick, then stick into each triangle and serve immediately.

French Country Terrine

This versatile terrine can be served in slices, used to fill sandwiches or cut into small cubes and threaded on to cocktail sticks with tiny gherkins or onions.

Makes 1 terrine or loaf

INGREDIENTS
450 g/1 lb leeks, trimmed, cut in half
   lengthways and washed
15 g/½ oz/1 tbsp butter
2–3 garlic cloves, finely chopped
1 kg/2¼ lb lean pork, well trimmed,
   cut into pieces
150 g/5 oz smoked streaky bacon
   rashers
7.5 ml/1½ tsp chopped fresh thyme
   or 5 ml/1 tsp dried thyme
2.5 ml/½ tsp dried sage
1.25 ml/¼ tsp grated nutmeg
2.5 ml/½ tsp quatre épices or allspice
2.5 ml/½ tsp salt
5 ml/1 tsp freshly ground black pepper
2 bay leaves
cherry tomatoes, to garnish

TO SERVE
French country bread or French stick,
   sliced and toasted
French grainy mustard
pickled gherkins
chicory leaves

COOK'S TIP
The pork can be minced in a hand mincer if you do not have a food processor. Alternatively, ask your butcher to coarsely mince a piece of pork leg or shoulder.

1 Thinly slice the leeks. In a large heavy saucepan, melt the butter and stir in the leeks. Cook over low heat, covered, for 10 minutes, stirring occasionally. Stir in the garlic and cook for 5–7 minutes longer, until the leeks are tender. Remove from the heat to cool.

2 Put the pork pieces in the bowl of a food processor (you may need to work in 2 or 3 batches) and process carefully until coarsely chopped. Do not over process. Transfer to a large bowl.

3 Reserve 2 or 3 rashers of bacon and process the remaining slices. Add to the pork mixture with the leeks, thyme, sage, quatre épices, nutmeg, salt and pepper. Using a wooden spoon or your hands, mix until well combined.

streaky bacon

pork

sage

grainy
mustard

leeks

quatre épices

butter

nutmeg   French bread

bay leaf   black pepper

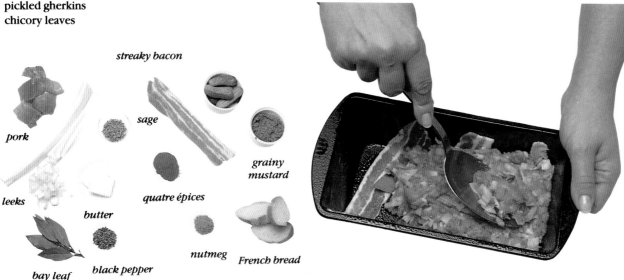

4 Preheat the oven to 180°C/350°F/ Gas 4. Grease a heavy, non-stick 1.5 litre/ 2½ pint/6¼ cup terrine or loaf tin. Drape the reserved bacon rashers diagonally across the tin, pressing into the corners. Put the bay leaves down the centre of the tin bottom, then spoon in the terrine mixture, pressing it into the sides and corners. Smooth the top of the terrine and then cover with foil.

5 Put the terrine in a roasting pan and pour in enough boiling water to come half way up the sides of the terrine. Bake for 1 ¼ hours. Cool completely. Place a foil-covered piece of board, cut to fit, on top of the terrine. Weigh it down with 2 heavy cans or weights and refrigerate overnight.

6 To serve, loosen the edges of the terrine with a knife and turn out onto a serving dish or cutting board. Scrape off any congealed fat or juices and cut into thin slices. Serve on chicory leaves or pieces of toasted French bread, spread with French grainy mustard and gherkins and garnished with cherry tomatoes.

Scandinavian Open Sandwiches

The Swedes and Danes are famous for their open sandwiches, which are often served as part of a *smörgåsbord* – a huge party buffet of both hot and cold dishes.

Makes 16 halves

INGREDIENTS
ROAST BEEF WITH HORSERADISH CREAM
45–60 ml/3–4 tbsp mayonnaise
15 ml/1 tbsp horseradish sauce
2–3 dashes hot pepper sauce
4 slices rye bread
4 slices very rare tender roast beef
diced sweet-and-sour pickled cucumber
watercress, to garnish

GRAVLAX WITH HONEY DILL MUSTARD SAUCE
30–45 ml/2–3 tbsp mayonnaise
10 ml/2 tsp Dijon mustard
15 ml/1 tbsp honey
5 ml/1 tsp vegetable oil
15 ml/1 tbsp chopped fresh dill
4 slices wholemeal bread
4–8 slices gravlax (cured salmon) depending on slice size
cucumber twists, to garnish
dill sprigs, to garnish

SMOKED CHICKEN AND AVOCADO WITH LIME
225 g/8 oz smoked chicken breast, skin removed
1 small ripe avocado, diced
50 ml/2 fl oz/¼ cup garlic mayonnaise
juice of ½ lime
4 slices pumpernickle or black rye bread
5–10 ml/1–2 tsp butter, softened
cucumber twists, to garnish
dill sprigs, to garnish
mint sprigs, to garnish

roast beef
pickled cucumber
watercress
rye bread
horseradish sauce
gravlax
avocado

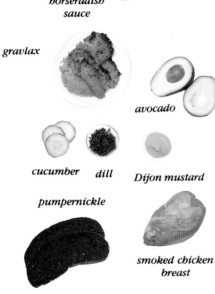

cucumber dill Dijon mustard
pumpernickle
smoked chicken breast

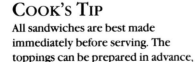

COOK'S TIP
All sandwiches are best made immediately before serving. The toppings can be prepared in advance, then assembled at the last minute.

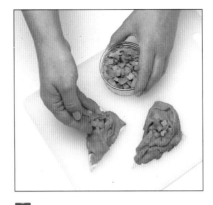

1 To make the Roast Beef with Horseradish, in a small bowl combine the mayonnaise and horseradish together with hot pepper sauce according to taste. Spread the rye bread slices with the horseradish sauce. Arrange the roast beef, in folds for a more attractive appearance, on the bread and cut each slice into 2 triangles. Sprinkle each with a little pickled cucumber, chopped into small cubes and garnish with a sprig of watercress.

2 For the Gravlax with Honey Dill Mustard, in a small bowl combine the mayonnaise, mustard, honey, oil and dill. Reserve 15–20 ml/1–2 tbsp for the garnish. Cut each slice of bread into 2 triangles and spread with the horseradish sauce. Arrange the gravlax on each triangle overlapping slightly, and garnish with cucumber slices and the remaining sauce.

3 For the Smoked Chicken and Avocado, slice the chicken breast. Toss the diced avocado in a bowl with the mayonnaise and lime juice until just blended.

4 Spread the pumpernickle bread slices with a little softened butter and cut each slice into 2 triangles. Arrange a few slices of chicken on the bread and top with a spoonful of the avocado mixture. Garnish with lime slices and a sprig of mint.

Greek Meze with Pitta Crisps

Meze are a selection of Greek hors d'oeuvres, and these three dips are quick and easy to make in a food processor and go well together – serve them with raw vegetables or these wonderful pitta crisps.

INGREDIENTS

FOR THE TZATZIKI (Makes about 750 ml/1¼ pints/3 cups)
1 large cucumber
5 ml/1 tsp salt
600 ml/1 pint/2½ cups thick Greek yogurt
1–2 garlic cloves, finely chopped
30–45 ml/2–3 tbsp chopped fresh mint or 1 tbsp dried mint
15–30 ml/1–2 tbsp virgin olive oil (optional)
mint sprigs, to garnish

FOR THE HUMMUS (Makes about 600 ml/1 pint/2½ cups)
1 × 525 g/19 oz can chickpeas
50 ml/3½ tbsp tahini (sesame paste)
50 ml/3½ tbsp freshly squeezed lemon juice
1–2 garlic cloves, crushed
salt
cayenne pepper, to taste
15–30 ml/1–2 tbsp olive oil
olive or sesame oil, for drizzling
15–30 ml/1–2 tbsp chopped fresh parsley or coriander

FOR THE SMOKY AUBERGINE DIP (Makes about 500 ml/16 fl oz/2 cups)
1 large aubergine (about 450 g/1 lb)
60 ml/4 tbsp freshly squeezed lemon juice
60 ml/4 tbsp tahini or mayonnaise
2–3 garlic cloves, chopped
salt
30 ml/2 tbsp virgin olive oil
30 ml/2 tbsp chopped fresh parsley

FOR THE PITTA CRISPS
4 large pitta breads
olive oil
dried oregano or herbes de Provence
salt

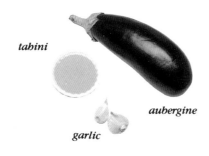

cucumber
yogurt
olive oil
mint
chickpeas
tahini
lemon
chopped parsley
cayenne pepper
tahini
aubergine
garlic

1 For the Tzatziki, peel the cucumber and cut lengthways into quarters. Cut out the seeds, chop finely and place in a colander. Sprinkle with the salt and allow to drain for about 1 hour. Pat dry with paper towels. Put the yogurt in a bowl and stir in the drained cucumber, garlic and mint. Slowly blend in the olive oil, if using. Spoon into a serving bowl, garnish with mint and refrigerate.

2 For the Hummus, drain the chickpeas, reserving the liquid. Set aside a few chickpeas for garnishing. Put the remainder in a food processor and add the tahini, lemon juice and garlic. Process until very smooth, scraping down the side of the bowl occasionally. Season with the salt and cayenne pepper and process to blend.

3 With the machine running, slowly pour in 15–30 ml/1–2 tbsp olive oil and some of the reserved chickpea liquid to thin the purée if necessary. Pour into a shallow serving bowl and spread it up the side of the bowl swirling with the back of a spoon. Pour a little extra olive oil or sesame oil in the centre, add the chickpeas and a sprinkle of cayenne pepper. Sprinkle with the chopped parsley or coriander.

4 For the Smoky Aubergine Dip, if possible, barbecue the aubergine over a charcoal fire for about 30 minutes. Alternatively, place on a rack with a tray placed below, in the centre of a preheated oven, 200°C/400°F/Gas 6. Bake for about 30 minutes or until soft, turning frequently. Remove from the oven. When cool enough to handle, scoop out the flesh into the bowl of a food processor. Add the lemon juice, tahini or mayonnaise, garlic, salt to taste, olive oil and 15 ml/1 tbsp of the parsley. Process for 1–2 minutes until very smooth, scraping the sides of the bowl once or twice. Pour into a shallow bowl and garnish with the remaining parsley.

5 For the Pitta Crisps, preheat the oven to 180°C/350°/Gas 4. Split the pittas in half lengthways to form two thin layers. Brush generously with olive oil and sprinkle with a little dried oregano or *herbes de Provence* and a pinch of salt. Cut each in half lengthways, then into triangles and place on 2 large baking sheets. Bake the pitta triangles for 15–20 minutes until golden and crisp. Cool on the baking sheets and then store in an airtight container until ready to serve.

COOK'S TIP

You can, of course, serve these dips with warmed pitta bread, but for parties these crisps are ideal because they don't spoil, and they are cooked in advance, so do make the extra effort – it's worth it!

Corn Fritters with Red Pepper Salsa

The salsa can also be served with grilled chicken or vegetable kebabs. Add the chillies slowly and according to your taste, as they can be very hot.

Makes about 48

INGREDIENTS
corn or other vegetable oil
2 × 225 g/8 oz frozen or canned
    sweetcorn kernals, drained
140 g/5 oz/1 cup plain flour
55 g/2 oz/½ cup cornmeal
250 ml/8 fl oz/1 cup milk
10 ml/2 tsp baking powder
10 ml/2 tsp sugar
5 ml/1 tsp salt
2.5 ml/½ tsp nutmeg
2.5 ml/½ tsp cayenne pepper
4 eggs, lightly beaten
coriander leaves, to garnish

FOR THE SALSA
115 g/4 oz cherry tomatoes, chopped
115 g/4 oz frozen or canned
    sweetcorn kernels, drained
1 red pepper, cored and finely
    chopped
½ small red onion, finely chopped
juice of 1 lemon
30 ml/2 tbsp olive oil
30 ml/2 tbsp chopped fresh coriander
1 to 2 fresh chillies, seeded and finely
    chopped
salt
2.5 ml/½ tsp sugar

red onion

sweetcorn

red pepper

egg

cornmeal

lemon

chilli

chopped coriander

milk

cherry tomatoes

olive oil

cayenne pepper

nutmeg

1 Prepare the Salsa at least 2 hours ahead. Combine the ingredients in a medium-sized bowl, crushing them lightly with the back of a spoon to release juices. Cover and refrigerate until ready to use.

2 In a medium-sized bowl combine 30 ml/2 tbsp of the oil with the sweetcorn, flour, cornmeal, milk, baking powder, sugar, salt, nutmeg, cayenne pepper and eggs, until just blended; do not overbeat. If the batter is too stiff stir in a little more milk or water.

3 In a large heavy-based frying pan, heat 1 cm/½ in oil until hot but not smoking. Drop tablespoonsful of batter into the hot oil and cook for 3 to 4 minutes until golden, turning once. Drain on paper towels. Arrange on baking sheets and keep warm for up to 1 hour in an oven, at 170°C/325°F/Gas 3.

4 Arrange the corn fritters on a serving plate. Top each with a spoonful of salsa and garnish with a coriander leaf. Serve hot or warm.

COOK'S TIP
The salsa can be made up to a day in advance. Keep in the fridge, covered.

Mini Sausage Rolls

These miniature versions of old-fashioned sausage rolls are always popular – the Parmesan cheese gives them an extra special flavour.

Makes about 48

INGREDIENTS
15 g/½ oz/1 tbsp butter
1 onion, finely chopped
350 g/12 oz good quality sausage meat
15 ml/1 tbsp dried mixed herbs such as oregano, thyme, sage, tarragon or dill
salt and pepper
25 g/1 oz finely chopped pistachio nuts (optional)
350 g/12 oz puff pastry
60–90 ml/4–6 tbsp freshly grated Parmesan cheese
1 egg, lightly beaten, for glazing
poppy seeds, sesame seeds, fennel seeds or aniseeds, for sprinkling

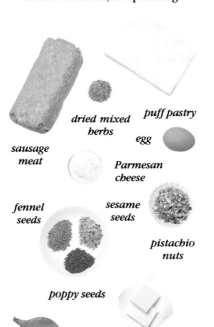

sausage meat *dried mixed herbs* *puff pastry* *egg* *Parmesan cheese* *fennel seeds* *sesame seeds* *pistachio nuts* *poppy seeds* *onion* *butter*

VARIATION

Filo pastry can be used instead of puff pastry for a very light effect. Depending on the size of the filo sheets, cut into 8 pieces 25 × 7.5 cm/ 10 × 3 in. Brush 4 of the sheets with a little melted butter or vegetable oil and place a second pastry sheet on top. Place one sausage log on each of the four layered sheets and roll up and bake as above.

1 In a small frying pan, over a medium heat, melt the butter. Add the onion and cook for about 5 minutes, until softened. Remove from the heat and cool. Put the onion, sausage meat, herbs, salt and pepper and nuts (if using) in a mixing bowl and stir together until blended.

2 Divide the sausage mixture into 4 equal portions and roll into thin sausages about 25 cm/10 in long. Set aside.

3 On a lightly floured surface, roll out the pastry to about 3 mm/⅛ in thick. Cut the pastry into 4 strips 25 × 7.5 cm/ 10 × 3 in long. Place a long sausage on each pastry strip and sprinkle each with a little Parmesan cheese.

4 Brush one long edge of each of the pastry strips with the egg glaze and roll up to enclose each sausage. Set them seam-side down and press gently to seal. Brush each with the egg glaze and sprinkle with one type of seeds. Repeat with remaining pastry strips and different seeds.

5 Preheat the oven to 220°C/425°F/ Gas 7. Lightly grease a large baking sheet. Cut each of the pastry logs into 2.5 cm/ 1 in lengths and arrange on the baking sheet. Bake for 15 minutes until the pastry is crisp and brown. Serve warm or at room temperature.

Smoked Trout Mousse in Cucumber Cups

This delicious creamy mousse can be made in advance and kept for 2–3 days in the refrigerator. Serve it in crunchy cucumber cups, or simply with crudités.

Makes about 24

INGREDIENTS
120 g/4 oz/⅔ cup cream cheese,
  softened
2 spring onions, chopped
15–30 ml/1–2 tbsp, chopped fresh dill
  or parsley
5 ml/1 tsp horseradish sauce
225 g/8 oz smoked trout fillets, flaked
  and any fine bones removed
30–60 ml/2–4 tbsp double cream
salt
cayenne pepper, to taste
2 cucumbers
dill sprigs, to garnish

spring onions

cucumber

smoked trout

double cream

cream cheese

cayenne pepper

horseradish sauce

dill

VARIATION
For Smoked Salmon Mousse use smoked salmon pieces instead of smoked trout.

1 Put the cream cheese, spring onions, dill and horseradish sauce into the bowl of a food processor and process until well blended. Add the trout and process until smooth, scraping down the side of the bowl once. With the machine running, pour in the cream until a soft mousse-like mixture forms. Season, turn into a bowl and refrigerate for 15 minutes.

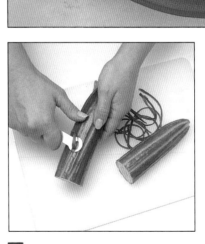

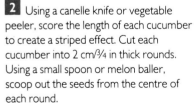

2 Using a canelle knife or vegetable peeler, score the length of each cucumber to create a striped effect. Cut each cucumber into 2 cm/¾ in thick rounds. Using a small spoon or melon baller, scoop out the seeds from the centre of each round.

3 Spoon the mousse into a piping bag fitted with a medium star nozzle and pipe swirls of the mixture into the cucumber rounds. Refrigerate until ready to serve. Garnish each with a small sprig of dill.

Carpaccio Rolls with Anchovy Mayonnaise

This famous hors d'oeuvre of raw beef makes an extravagant but delicious treat.

Makes about 24

INGREDIENTS
225 g/8 oz fillet of beef, cut from the
  narrow end, and frozen for 1 hour
60 ml/4 tbsp virgin olive oil
15 ml/1 tbsp lemon juice
freshly ground black pepper
rocket or flat-leaf parsley, to garnish
capers, to garnish

FOR THE ANCHOVY MAYONNAISE
4–6 anchovy fillets
250 ml/8 fl oz/1 cup home-made or
  good quality mayonnaise
15 ml/1 tbsp capers, rinsed, drained
  and chopped
1 small garlic clove, crushed
30 ml/2 tbsp freshly grated Parmesan
  cheese

endive leaves or short celery sticks, to
  serve

lemon *Parmesan cheese*

fillet of beef

anchovy fillets

virgin olive oil

mayonnaise

capers *garlic*

1 For the Anchovy Mayonnaise, in a medium-sized bowl, mash the anchovy fillets with a fork, then beat in the mayonnaise, capers, garlic and Parmesan cheese until well blended.

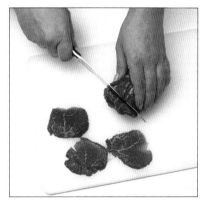

2 Slice the beef into as many wafer-thin pieces as possible and arrange flat on a baking sheet. Brush each piece with the olive oil and sprinkle with a little lemon juice and black pepper.

3 Place about half a teaspoon of Anchovy Mayonnaise in the centre of each beef slice and fold into quarters, or roll up.

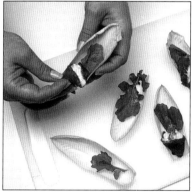

4 To serve, place a rocket leaf at the bottom of an endive leaf and place a rolled or folded up slice of beef on top. Sprinkle with a few capers if you like. If you prefer, skewer each beef parcel with a cocktail stick and serve on its own.

Spicy Crab Cakes

These are miniature versions of a classic American speciality. Use fresh crab meat if your budget allows.

Makes about 30

INGREDIENTS

225 g/8 oz crab meat, drained and
  picked over
75 g/3 oz/1½ cups fresh white
  breadcrumbs
2 spring onions, finely chopped
15–30 ml/1–2 tbsp chopped fresh dill
  or parsley
1 egg, lightly beaten
50 ml/2 fl oz/¼ cup mayonnaise
15 ml/1 tbsp Dijon mustard
15–30 ml/1–2 tbsp lemon juice
salt
1 small green chilli, seeded and
  chopped (optional)
2–3 dashes hot pepper sauce
fine dried breadcrumbs, for coating
vegetable oil, for frying

FOR THE SEAFOOD COCKTAIL SAUCE
115 ml/4 fl oz/½ cup horseradish
  sauce
15–30 ml/1–2 tbsp mayonnaise
50 ml/2 fl oz/¼ cup tomato ketchup
lemon juice, to taste

crab meat   breadcrumbs

chilli pepper

egg   mayonnaise   Dijon mustard

parsley   tomato ketchup   horseradish sauce

hot pepper sauce   spring onions

lemon

1 For the Seafood Cocktail Sauce, in a small bowl, combine all the ingredients and mix well. Cover and refrigerate. For the crab cakes, in a large bowl, combine all the ingredients, except the oil and dried breadcrumbs.

2 Using a small ice-cream scoop or teaspoon, form the mixture into walnut-sized balls. Place on a baking sheet.

3 Put the dried breadcrumbs in a shallow plate and coat the crab balls, a few at a time, rolling to cover completely. Place on a baking sheet and flatten each ball slightly until 1 cm/½ in thick. Refrigerate for 30 minutes or longer.

4 In a large heavy frying pan heat 1 cm/½ in oil, until hot but not smoking. Fry the crab cakes, in batches, for about 2 minutes until crisp and golden, turning once. Serve hot or warm with the sauce.

Smoked Salmon Nests on Wild Rice Pancakes

The nutty flavour of wild rice provides a perfect foil to the smoky richness of the salmon, in this elegant hors d'oeuvre.

Makes about 24

INGREDIENTS
225 g/8 oz smoked salmon
45–60 ml/3–4 tbsp creamed
    horseradish sauce
fresh chives or dill, to garnish

FOR THE WILD RICE PANCAKES
70 g/2½ oz/½ cup plain flour
salt and white pepper
1 egg, lightly beaten
60 ml/2 fl oz/¼ cup milk
200 g/7 oz/1⅓ cups cooked wild rice
30 ml/2 tbsp chopped chives or dill
vegetable oil, for frying

vegetable oil

milk

horseradish sauce

egg

plain flour

chives

smoked salmon   *wild rice*

1 Prepare the Wild Rice Pancakes, sift the flour, salt and pepper into a medium-sized bowl and make a well in the centre. Put the egg and milk in the well and, using a wire whisk or electric beater on slow speed, gradually bring in the flour from the edges to form a smooth batter. Stir in the wild rice and chives or dill.

VARIATION
The same effect can be achieved more simply by making little bread rounds instead of pancakes. Cut out 5 cm/2 in rounds from white or brown sliced bread and toast briefly on both sides before adding the topping.

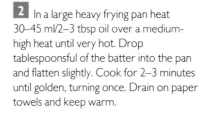

2 In a large heavy frying pan heat 30–45 ml/2–3 tbsp oil over a medium-high heat until very hot. Drop tablespoonsful of the batter into the pan and flatten slightly. Cook for 2–3 minutes until golden, turning once. Drain on paper towels and keep warm.

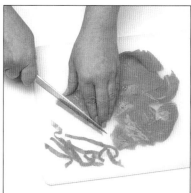

3 With a sharp knife, cut the smoked salmon into thin strips. Spoon a little horseradish cream onto each pancake and top with a pile of salmon strips twisting to form a nest. If you like, garnish with extra dollops of horseradish cream and fresh chives or dill.

Foie Gras Pâté in Filo Cups

This is an extravagantly rich hors d'oeuvre – save it for a special occasion.

Makes about 24

INGREDIENTS
3–6 sheets fresh or defrosted filo
   pastry
45 g/1½ oz/3 tbsp butter, melted
225 g/8 oz tinned foie gras pâté or
   other fine liver pâté, at room
   temperature
60 g/2 oz/4 tbsp butter, softened
30–45 ml/2–3 tbsp Cognac or brandy
   (optional)
chopped pistachios, to garnish

filo pastry

foie gras pâté

pistachio nuts

butter

Cognac

COOK'S TIP

The pâté and pastry are best eaten soon after preparation. If preparing ahead and refrigerating, be sure to bring back to room temperature before serving.

1 Preheat the oven to 200°C/400°F/ Gas 6. Grease a bun tray with 24 × 4 cm/ 1½ in cups. Stack the filo sheets on a work surface and cut into 6 cm/2½ in squares. Cover with a damp towel.

2 Keeping the rest of the filo squares covered, place one square on a work surface and brush lightly with melted butter, then turn and brush the other side.

Butter a second square and place it over the first at an angle. Butter a third square and place at an angle over the first two sheets to form an uneven edge.

3 Press the layers into the cup of the bun tray. Continue with the remaining pastry and butter until all the cups are filled.

4 Bake the filo cups for 4–6 minutes until crisp and golden, then remove and cool in the pan for 5 minutes. Carefully remove each filo cup to a wire rack and cool completely.

5 In a small bowl, beat the pâté with the softened butter until smooth and well blended. Add the Cognac or brandy to taste, if using. Spoon into a piping bag fitted with a medium star nozzle and pipe a swirl into each cup. Sprinkle with pistachio nuts. Refrigerate until ready to serve.

Grilled Asparagus Tips with Easy Hollandaise Sauce

Delicate asparagus tips and buttery rich Hollandaise Sauce make a classic combination and a delicious treat.

Makes 24

INGREDIENTS
24 large asparagus spears
oil, for brushing
freshly grated Parmesan cheese, for
  sprinkling

FOR THE HOLLANDAISE SAUCE
175 g/6 oz/¾ cup butter, cut into
  pieces
2 egg yolks
15 ml/1 tbsp lemon juice
15 ml/1 tbsp water
salt and cayenne pepper

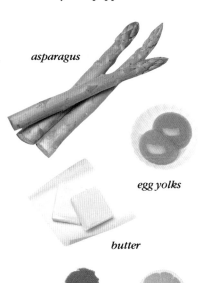

asparagus

egg yolks

butter

cayenne pepper

lemon

lemon juice

COOK'S TIP
Keep the Hollandaise Sauce warm by storing it in a vacuum flask until ready to serve.

1 Prepare the Hollandaise Sauce, melt the butter in a small saucepan and skim off any foam which bubbles to the top.

2 Put the egg yolks, lemon juice and water into a blender or a food processor. Season with salt and cayenne pepper and blend or process to mix. With the machine running, slowly pour in the hot butter in a thin stream; do not pour in the milky solids on the bottom of the pan.

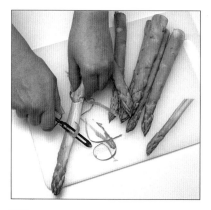

3 Using a vegetable peeler, peel the asparagus spears. Cut off the stalks to leave tips of about 12.5 cm/5 in.

4 Cook the tips in boiling salted water for 2–3 minutes until just tender; do not overcook. Refresh under cold water to stop them cooking, then cover until ready to serve.

5 Preheat the grill. Line a baking sheet with foil and brush each asparagus tip with a little oil. Sprinkle each tip with a little Parmesan cheese, then grill for 2–3 minutes, turning once. Arrange the asparagus on a plate, and serve with the Hollandaise Sauce for dipping.

VARIATION

Wrap each asparagus tip in a thin strip of bacon or Parma ham and brush with oil before grilling. If you like cut the remainder of the asparagus spears into 7.5 cm/3 in pieces and grill them, for slightly longer, as well.

Marinated Mussels

This is an ideal recipe to prepare and arrange well in advance. Remove from the refrigerator 15 minutes before serving to allow the flavours to develop.

Makes 48

INGREDIENTS

1 kilo/2.2 lb mussels, large if possible
175 ml/6 fl oz/¾ cup dry white wine
1 garlic clove, well crushed
freshly ground black pepper
120 ml/4 fl oz/½ cup olive oil
50 ml/2 fl oz/¼ cup lemon juice
5 ml/1 tsp hot chilli flakes
2.5 ml/½ tsp mixed spice
15 ml/1 tbsp Dijon mustard
10 ml/2 tsp sugar
5 ml/1 tsp salt
15–30 ml/1–2 tbsp chopped fresh dill
  or coriander
15 ml/1 tbsp capers, diced, drained
  and chopped if large

lemon　　　*mussels*

sugar

olive oil

mixed spice　　*capers*

garlic

Dijon mustard

dill

hot chilli flakes

Mussels can be prepared ahead and marinated for up to 24 hours. To serve, arrange the mussel shells on a bed of crushed ice, well-washed seaweed or even coarse salt to stop them wobbling on the plate.

1 With a stiff kitchen brush, under running cold water, scrub the mussels to remove any sand and barnacles; pull out and remove any beards. Discard any open shells that will not shut when tapped.

2 In a large casserole or saucepan over high heat, bring to the boil the white wine with the garlic and freshly ground black pepper. Add the mussels and cover. Reduce the heat to medium and simmer for 2 to 4 minutes until the shells open, stirring occasionally.

3 In a large bowl combine the olive oil, lemon juice, chilli flakes, mixed spice, Dijon mustard, sugar, salt, chopped dill or coriander and capers.

4 Discard any mussels with closed shells. With a small sharp knife, carefully remove remaining mussels from their shells, reserving 48 shells for serving. Add the mussels to the marinade. Toss the mussels to coat well, then cover and refrigerate for 6 to 8 hours or overnight, stirring gently from time to time.

5 With a teaspoon, place one mussel with a little marinade in each shell. Arrange on a platter and cover until ready to serve.

A Trio of Tartlets

Tender pastry topped with luscious ingredients
always look irresistible and taste even better.
Vary the toppings according to the occasion.

Makes about 24

INGREDIENTS
175 g/6 oz/1⅓ cups flour
2.5 ml/½ tsp salt
75 g/3 oz/6 tbsp butter, cut into
  pieces
1 egg yolk beaten with 30–45 ml/2–3
  tbsp cold water

FOR THE SCRAMBLED EGG AND CAVIAR
15 ml/1 tbsp butter
2 eggs, lightly beaten
salt and white pepper
15 ml/1 tbsp double cream or crème
  fraîche
15–30 ml/1–2 tbsp caviar or lumpfish
  caviar

FOR THE SMOKED SALMON AND LEEK
120 ml/4 oz/½ cup double cream
1 leek, split lengthways, washed and
  thinly sliced
salt and freshly ground black pepper
pinch of nutmeg
115 g/4 oz smoked salmon, sliced very
  thinly
dill sprigs, to garnish

FOR THE ASPARAGUS AND BRIE
15 ml/1 tbsp butter
6 asparagus stalks cut into 4 cm/1½ in
  pieces
salt
50 g/2 oz Brie, rind removed and
  sliced

flour

salt

eggs

caviar

*double
cream*

butter

*smoked
salmon*

leek

nutmeg

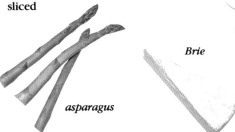
asparagus

Brie

1 Prepare the pastry, put the flour, salt and butter into the bowl of a food processor and process carefully, until the mixture resembles fine crumbs. Reserve 15 ml/1 tbsp of the egg mixture. With the processor running, pour in the remaining egg mixture until the dough just begins to come together (do not allow it to form a ball or it may toughen). If the dough is too dry add a little more water and process briefly again. Turn the dough on to a piece of clear film and use the film to push it together and flatten to form a disc shape. Wrap tightly, refrigerate for 1½ hours.

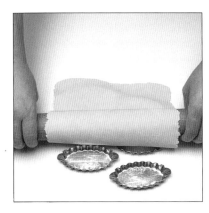

2 On a lightly floured surface, roll out the pastry to a 3 mm/⅛ in thickness. Lay out about 12 5 cm/2 in tartlet tins. Lay the pastry over the tins and press out. Reroll the trimmings and repeat. Line 24 cases, then prick the bases with a fork and refrigerate for 30 minutes.

3 Preheat the oven to 190°C/375°F/ Gas 5. Put a small piece of crumbled foil into each case and place on a baking sheet. Bake for 6–8 minutes until the edges are golden. Remove the foil and brush each pastry base with a little of the reserved egg mixture. Bake for 2 minutes until dry. Transfer to a wire rack to cool.

4 Prepare the fillings, for the Scrambled Egg and Caviar, melt the butter in a small frying pan over medium-low heat. Season the eggs with salt and white pepper and add to the pan. Cook the eggs slowly, stirring constantly, until smooth and just set. Remove from the heat and stir in the cream or crème fraîche. Spoon into 8 of the cases. Just before serving, garnish each tartlet with a pinch of caviar. Serve warm or at room temperature.

5 For the Smoked Salmon and Leek, bring the cream to a simmer in a medium saucepan over medium heat. Add the leeks and cook, stirring frequently, until just tender and the cream is completely reduced. Season with salt, pepper and a pinch of nutmeg. Spoon into 8 of the cases and top with smoked salmon strips and sprigs of dill just before serving. Serve warm or at room temperature.

6 For the Asparagus and Brie, melt the butter in a medium-sized frying pan over medium-high heat. Add the asparagus pieces and stir-fry for 2–3 minutes until tender. Divide among the remaining tartlets and sprinkle each with a little salt. Divide the Brie among the tartlets. Just before serving, return to the oven for 1–2 minutes until the Brie softens. Serve straight away before the cheese hardens.

COOK'S TIP

If you do not have 24 tartlet tins, you will need to work in batches. Divide the dough in half or quarters and refrigerate the portion you are not using immediately.

Hazelnut Sablés with Goat's Cheese and Strawberries

Sablés are little French biscuits, made from egg yolk and butter. Crisp and slightly sweet, they contrast perfectly with the tangy goat's cheese and juicy strawberries.

Makes about 24

INGREDIENTS
75 g/3 oz/6 tbsp butter, at room temperature
140 g/5 oz/1 cup plain flour
75 g/3 oz/6 tbsp blanched hazelnuts, lightly toasted and ground
30 ml/2 tbsp caster sugar
2 egg yolks beaten with 30–45 ml/2–3 tbsp water
120 g/4 oz goat's cheese
4–6 large strawberries, cut into small pieces
chopped hazelnuts, to decorate

1 Make the pastry, put the butter, flour, ground hazelnuts, sugar and beaten egg yolks into the bowl of a food processor and process until a smooth dough forms.

goat's cheese strawberries
ground hazelnuts
chopped hazelnuts butter
egg yolks
flour

VARIATION

These sablés are ideal served with fruit. Beat 75 g/3 oz cream cheese with 15 ml/1 tbsp icing sugar and a little lemon or orange zest. Spread a little on the sablé and top with a few pieces of sliced kiwi fruit, peach, nectarine and a few raspberries or cut-up strawberries.

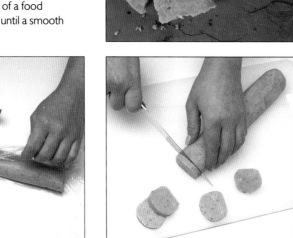

2 Scrape the dough out on to a sheet of clear film and use the film to shape the dough into a log about 4 cm/1½ in in diameter. Wrap tightly and refrigerate for 2 hours or overnight until very firm.

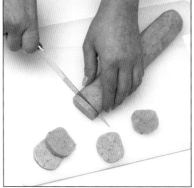

3 Preheat the oven to 200°C/400°F/Gas 6 and line a large baking sheet with non-stick baking parchment. With a sharp knife slice the dough into 5 mm/¼ in thick rounds and arrange on the baking sheet. Bake for 7–10 minutes until golden brown. Remove to a wire rack to cool and crisp slightly.

4 On a plate, crumble the goat's cheese into small pieces. Mound a little goat's cheese on to each sablé, top with a piece of strawberry and sprinkle with a few hazelnuts. Serve warm.

Rich Chocolate and Fruit Fondue

This sumptuous fruit fondue, with its rich, delicious sauce, makes a lavish finish to a party.

Makes 350 ml/12 fl oz/1¹/₂ cups

INGREDIENTS
a selection of mixed fruit, such as kumquats, apple, peach and pear slices, banana slices, clementine segments, seedless grapes, cherries, peeled lychees, mango and papaya cubes, cut figs and plums
lemon juice

FOR THE CHOCOLATE
225 g/8 oz good quality plain chocolate, chopped
30 ml/2 tbsp golden syrup
120 ml/4 fl oz/¹/₂ cup whipping cream
30—45 ml/2—3 tbsp brandy or orange-liqueur

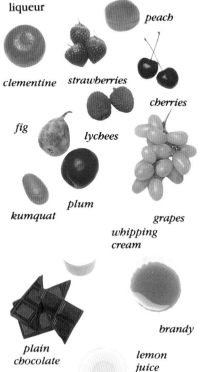

peach

clementine   strawberries

cherries

fig   lychees

plum

kumquat

grapes

whipping cream

plain chocolate

brandy

lemon juice

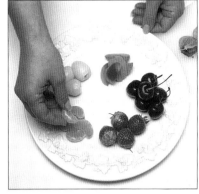

1 Arrange the fruits in an attractive pattern on a large serving dish. Brush any cut-up fruit such as apples, pears or banana with lemon juice to prevent darkening. Cover and refrigerate until ready to serve.

2 In a medium-sized saucepan over medium-low heat, combine the chopped chocolate, golden syrup and whipping cream. Stir until the chocolate is melted and smooth. Remove from the heat and stir in the brandy or liqueur. Poor into a serving bowl and serve with the chilled fruits and cocktail sticks.

VARIATION
You could also use small biscuits for dipping as well as, or instead of, the pieces of fruit.

Prawn Toasts

These crunchy sesame-topped toasts are simple to prepare using a food processor for the prawn paste.

Makes 64

INGREDIENTS
225 g/8 oz cooked, shelled prawns,
    well drained and dried
1 egg white
2 spring onions, chopped
5 ml/1 tsp chopped fresh root ginger
1 garlic clove, chopped
5 ml/1 tsp cornflour
2.5 ml/½ tsp salt
2.5 ml/½ tsp sugar
2–3 dashes hot pepper sauce
8 slices firm textured white bread
60–75 ml/4–5 tbsp sesame seeds
vegetable oil, for frying
spring onion pompom, to garnish

bread

vegetable oil

egg white

sesame seeds

root ginger

sugar

prawns

cornflour

garlic

spring onions

hot pepper sauce

1 Put the first 9 ingredients in the bowl of a food processor and process until the mixture forms a smooth paste, scraping down the side of the bowl occasionally.

2 Spread the prawn paste evenly over the bread slices, then sprinkle over the sesame seeds, pressing to make them stick. Remove the crusts, then cut each slice diagonally into 4 triangles, then cut each in half again to make 64 in total.

3 Heat 5 cm/2 in vegetable oil in a heavy saucepan or wok, until hot but not smoking. Fry the prawn-coated triangles for 30–60 seconds, turning once. Drain on paper towels and serve hot.

COOK'S TIP

You can prepare these in advance and heat them up in a hot oven before serving. Make sure they are crisp and properly heated through though, they won't be nearly as enjoyable if there's no crunch!

Thai-fried Vegetables in Wonton Cups

These crispy cups are an ideal way to serve stir-fried vegetables; use your imagination to vary the fillings.

Makes 24

INGREDIENTS

30 ml/2 tbsp vegetable oil, plus extra for greasing
24 small wonton wrappers
120 ml/4 fl oz/½ cup Hoi Sin sauce or plum sauce (optional)
5 ml/1 tsp sesame oil
1 garlic clove, finely chopped
1 cm/½ in piece fresh root ginger, finely chopped
5 cm/2 in piece of lemon grass, crushed
6–8 asparagus spears, cut into 3 cm/ 1¼ in pieces
8–10 baby sweetcorn, cut in half lengthways
1 small red pepper, seeded and cut into short slivers
15–30 ml/1–2 tbsp sugar
30 ml/2 tbsp soy sauce
juice of 1 lime
5–10 ml/1–2 tsp Chinese-style chilli sauce (or to taste)
1 tsp *huac nam* or Thai or other fish sauce

3 Add the sugar, soy sauce, lime juice, chilli sauce and fish sauce and toss well to coat. Stir-fry for 30 seconds longer.

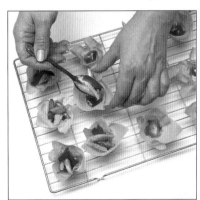

4 Spoon an equal amount of vegetable mixture into each of the prepared wonton cups and serve hot.

lemon grass

red pepper

Hoi Sin sauce

wonton wrappers

baby sweetcorn

vegetable oil

asparagus

sesame oil

soy sauce

garlic

lime

1 Preheat the oven to 180°C/350°F/ Gas 4. Lightly grease 24 4 cm/1½ in bun tins. Press 1 wonton wrapper into each cup, turning the edges up to form a cup shape. Bake for 8–10 minutes, until crisp and golden. Carefully remove to a wire rack to cool. If you like, brush each cup with a little Hoi Sin or plum sauce (this will help keep the cups crisp if preparing them in advance).

2 In a wok or large frying pan, heat 30 ml/2 tbsp vegetable oil and the sesame oil until very hot. Add the garlic, ginger and lemon grass and stir-fry for 15 seconds until fragrant. Add the asparagus, sweetcorn and red pepper pieces and stir-fry for 2 minutes until tender crisp.

Chicken Satay with Peanut Sauce

These skewers of marinated chicken can be prepared in advance and served at room temperature. Beef, pork or even lamb fillet can be used instead of chicken if you prefer.

Makes about 24

INGREDIENTS
450 g/1 lb boneless, skinless chicken
   breasts
sesame seeds, for sprinkling
red pepper, to garnish

FOR THE MARINADE
90 ml/6 tbsp vegetable oil
60 ml/4 tbsp tamari or light soy sauce
60 ml/4 tbsp fresh lime juice
2.5 cm/½ in piece fresh root ginger,
   peeled and chopped
3–4 garlic cloves
30 ml/2 tbsp light brown sugar
5 ml/1 tsp Chinese-style chilli sauce or
   1 small red chilli pepper, seeded
   and chopped
30 ml/2 tbsp fresh chopped coriander

FOR THE PEANUT SAUCE
30 ml/2 tbsp smooth peanut butter
30 ml/2 tbsp soy sauce
15 ml/1 tbsp sesame or vegetable oil
2 spring onions, chopped
2 garlic cloves
15–30 ml/1–2 tbsp fresh lime or
   lemon juice
15 ml/1 tbsp brown sugar

1 Prepare the marinade. Place all the marinade ingredients in the bowl of a food processor or blender and process until smooth and well blended, scraping down sides of the bowl once. Pour into a shallow dish and set aside.

2 Into the same food processor or blender, put all the Peanut Sauce ingredients and process until well blended. If the sauce is too thick add a little water and process again. Pour into a small bowl and cover until ready to serve.

4 Add the chicken pieces to the marinade in the dish. Toss well to coat, cover and marinate for 3–4 hours in a cool place, or overnight in a refrigerator.

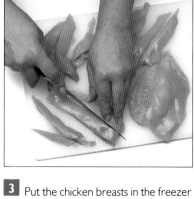

3 Put the chicken breasts in the freezer for 5 minutes to firm. Slice the chicken breasts in half horizontally, then into thin strips. Cut the strips into 2 cm/¾ in pieces.

5 Preheat the grill. Line a baking sheet with foil and brush lightly with oil. Thread 2–3 pieces of marinated chicken on to skewers and sprinkle with the sesame seeds. Grill for 4–5 minutes until golden, turning once. Serve with the Peanut Sauce, and a garnish of red pepper strips.

COOK'S TIP
When using metal skewers, look for flat ones which prevent the food from spinning around. If using wooden skewers, be sure to soak them in cold water for at least 30 minutes, to prevent them from burning.

red pepper *ginger* *vegetable oil*
brown sugar *soy sauce* *lime*
coriander *chilli sauce* *spring onions*
garlic *sesame oil* *sesame seeds* *chicken breast*

Lamb Tikka

Creamy yogurt and nuts go wonderfully with the spices in these little Indian meatballs.

Makes about 20

INGREDIENTS
450 g/1 lb lamb fillet
2 spring onions, chopped

FOR THE MARINADE
350 ml/12 fl oz/1½ cups natural
    yogurt
15 ml/1 tbsp ground almonds,
    cashews or peanuts
15 ml/1 tbsp vegetable oil
2–3 garlic cloves, finely chopped
juice of 1 lemon
5 ml/1 tsp garam masala or curry
    powder
2.5 ml/½ tsp ground cardamom
1.25 ml/¼ tsp cayenne pepper
15–30 ml/1–2 tbsp chopped fresh
    mint

spring onions

lamb fillet *ground almonds* *natural yogurt*

lemon *garam masala* *cayenne pepper*

ground cardamom *vegetable oil*

garlic *mint*

1 Prepare the marinade, in a medium-sized bowl, stir together all the ingredients except the lamb. In a separate small bowl, reserve about 120 ml/4 fl oz/½ cup of the mixture to use as a dipping sauce.

2 Cut the lamb into small pieces and put in the bowl of a food processor with the spring onions. Process, using the pulse action until the meat is finely chopped. Add 30–45 ml/2–3 tbsp of the marinade and process again.

3 Test to see if the mixture holds together by pinching a little between your fingertips. Add a little more marinade if necessary, but do not make the mixture too wet and soft.

4 With moistened palms, form the meat mixture into slightly oval-shaped balls about 4 cm/1½ in long and arrange in a shallow baking dish. Spoon over the remaining marinade and refrigerate the meat balls for 8–10 hours or overnight.

5 Preheat the grill and line a baking sheet with foil. Thread each meatball on to a skewer and arrange on the baking sheet. Grill for 4–5 minutes, turning occasionally, until crisp and golden on all sides. Serve with the reserved marinade/dipping sauce.

Smoked Duck Wontons with Spicy Mango Sauce

These Chinese-style wontons are easy to make using ready-cooked smoked duck or chicken, or even left-overs from the Sunday roast.

Makes about 40

INGREDIENTS
15 ml/1 tbsp light soy sauce
5 ml/1 tsp sesame oil
2 spring onions, finely chopped
grated zest of ½ orange
5 ml/1 tsp brown sugar
275 g/10 oz/1½ cups chopped
    smoked duck
about 40 small wonton wrappers
15 ml/1 tbsp vegetable oil

FOR THE SPICY MANGO SAUCE
30 ml/2 tbsp vegetable oil
5 ml/1 tsp ground cumin
2.5 ml/½ tsp ground cardamom
1.25 ml/¼ tsp ground cinnamon
250 ml/8 fl oz/1 cup mango purée
    (about 1 large mango)
15 ml/1 tbsp clear honey
2.5 ml/½ tsp Chinese chilli sauce (or
    to taste)
15 ml/1 tbsp cider vinegar
snipped fresh chives, to garnish

1 Prepare the sauce. In a medium-sized saucepan, heat the oil over medium-low heat. Add the spices and cook for about 3 minutes, stirring constantly.

2 Stir in the mango purée, honey, chilli sauce and vinegar. Remove from the heat and cool. Pour into a bowl and cover until ready to serve.

3 Prepare the wonton filling. In a large bowl, mix together the soy sauce, sesame oil, spring onions, orange zest and brown sugar until well blended. Add the duck and toss to coat well.

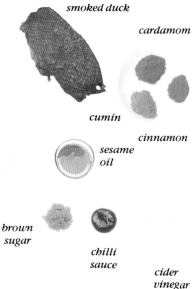

smoked duck
cardamom
cumin
cinnamon
sesame oil

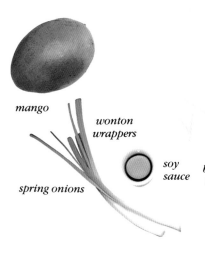

mango
wonton wrappers
spring onions
soy sauce
brown sugar
chilli sauce
cider vinegar

4 Place a teaspoonful of the duck mixture in the centre of each wonton wrapper. Brush the edges lightly with water and then draw them up to the centre, twisting to seal and forming a pouch shape.

5 Preheat the oven to 190°F/375°C/Gas 6. Line a large baking sheet with foil and brush lightly with oil. Arrange the wontons on the baking sheet and bake for 10–12 minutes until crisp and golden. Serve with the Spicy Mango Sauce. If you wish, tie each wonton with a fresh chive.

Tandoori Chicken Sticks

This aromatic chicken dish is traditionally baked in a special clay oven called a tandoor.

Makes about 25

INGREDIENTS
450 g/1 lb boneless, skinless chicken
   breasts

FOR THE CORIANDER YOGURT
250 ml/8 fl oz/1 cup natural yogurt
30 ml/2 tbsp whipping cream
½ cucumber, peeled, seeded and
   finely chopped
15–30 ml/1–2 tbsp fresh chopped
   coriander or mint
salt and freshly ground black pepper

FOR THE MARINADE
175 ml/6 fl oz/¾ cup natural yogurt
5 ml/1 tsp garam masala or curry
   powder
1.25 ml/¼ tsp ground cumin
1.25 ml/¼ tsp ground coriander
1.25 ml/¼ tsp cayenne pepper (or to
   taste)
5 ml/1 tsp tomato purée
1–2 garlic cloves, finely chopped
2.5 cm/½ in piece fresh root ginger,
   peeled and finely chopped
grated zest and juice of ½ lemon
15–30 ml/1–2 tbsp fresh chopped
   coriander or mint

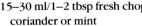
chicken breast

cumin
root ginger
garam masala
whipping cream
tomato purée
garlic
lemon
cucumber
natural yogurt

1 Prepare the Coriander Yogurt. Combine all the ingredients in a bowl and season with salt and freshly ground black pepper. Cover and refrigerate until ready to serve.

2 Prepare the marinade. Place all the ingredients in the bowl of a food processor, and process until smooth. Pour into a shallow dish.

3 Freeze the chicken breasts for 5 minutes to firm, then slice in half horizontally. Cut the slices into 2 cm/¾ in strips and add to the marinade. Toss to coat well. Cover and refrigerate for 6–8 hours or overnight.

4 Preheat the grill and line a baking sheet with foil. Using a slotted spoon, remove the chicken from the marinade and arrange the pieces in a single layer on the baking sheet. Scrunch up the chicken slightly so it makes wavy shapes. Grill for 4–5 minutes until brown and just cooked, turning once. Thread 1–2 pieces on to cocktail sticks or short skewers and serve with the yogurt dip.

Glazed Spare Ribs

These delicious sticky ribs are easy to eat with fingers once the little bones are cleaned away at one end to provide "handles".

Makes about 25

INGREDIENTS

1 kg/2¼ lb meaty pork spare ribs, cut into 5 cm/2 in lengths
175 ml/6 fl oz/¾ cup tomato ketchup or mild chilli sauce
30–45 ml/2–3 tbsp soy sauce
30–45 ml/2–3 tbsp clear honey
2 garlic cloves, finely chopped
50 ml/2 fl oz/¼ cup orange juice
1.25 ml/¼ tsp cayenne pepper (or to taste)
1.25 ml/¼ tsp Chinese five-spice powder
1–2 star anise

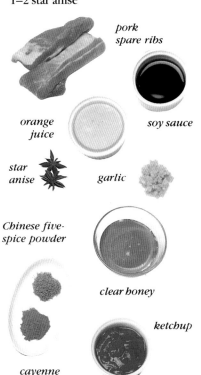

pork spare ribs
orange juice
soy sauce
star anise
garlic
Chinese five-spice powder
clear honey
ketchup
cayenne pepper

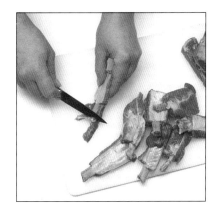

1 Using a small sharp knife, scrape away about 5 mm/¼ in of meat from one end of each tiny spare rib to serve as a little "handle".

2 In a large bowl or shallow baking dish, mix together the ketchup or chilli sauce, soy sauce, honey, garlic, orange juice, cayenne pepper, Chinese five-spice powder and star anise until well blended. Add the ribs and toss to coat. Cover and refrigerate for 6–8 hours or overnight.

3 Preheat the oven to 180°C/350°F/ Gas 4. Line a baking sheet with foil and arrange the spare ribs in a single layer, spooning over any remaining marinade.

4 Bake uncovered, basting occasionally, for 1 to 1½ hours, or until the ribs are well browned and glazed. Serve warm or at room temperature.

Sushi-style Tuna Cubes

These tasty tuna cubes are easier to prepare than classic Japanese sushi but retain the same fresh taste.

Makes about 24

INGREDIENTS
675 g/1½ lb fresh tuna steak,
  2 cm/¾ in thick
1 large red pepper, seeded and cut
  into 2 cm/¾ in pieces
sesame seeds, for sprinkling

FOR THE MARINADE
15–30 ml/1–2 tbsp lemon juice
2.5 ml/½ tsp salt
2.5 ml/½ tsp sugar
2.5 ml/½ tsp wasabi paste
120 ml/4 fl oz/½ cup olive or
  vegetable oil

FOR THE SOY DIPPING SAUCE
100 ml/3½ fl oz/2 cups soy sauce
15 ml/1 tbsp rice wine vinegar
5 ml/1 tsp lemon juice
1–2 spring onions, finely chopped
5 ml/1 tsp sugar
2–3 dashes Asian hot chilli oil or hot
  pepper sauce

fresh tuna

soy sauce

coriander   *olive oil*

red pepper   *sesame seeds*

wasabi paste   *lemon juice*   *vinegar*

pepper sauce   *sugar*   *spring onions*

1 Cut the tuna into 2.5 cm/1 in pieces and arrange them in a single layer in a large non-corrosive baking dish.

3 Meanwhile, prepare the Soy Dipping Sauce. Combine all the ingredients in a small bowl and stir until well blended. Cover until ready to serve.

2 Prepare the marinade. In a small bowl, stir the lemon juice with the salt, sugar and wasabi paste. Slowly whisk in the oil until well blended and slightly

4 Preheat the grill and line a baking sheet with foil. Thread a cube of tuna then a piece of pepper on to each skewer and arrange on the baking sheet.

creamy. Stir in the coriander. Pour over the tuna cubes and toss to coat. Cover and marinate for about 40 minutes in a cool place.

5 Sprinkle with sesame seeds and grill for 3–5 minutes, turning once or twice, until just beginning to colour but still pink inside. Serve with the Soy Dipping Sauce.

COOK'S TIP
Wasabi is a hot, pungent Japanese horseradish available in powder form and as paste in a tube from gourmet and Japanese food shops.

Bombay Prawns

These larger prawns are expensive, so save this dish for a special occasion.

Makes 24

INGREDIENTS
175 ml/6 fl oz/¾ cup olive oil
5 ml/1 tsp ground turmeric (or to taste)
5 ml/1 tsp ground cumin
5 ml/1 tsp garam masala or curry powder
2.5 ml/½ tsp salt
2.5 ml/½ tsp cayenne pepper (or to taste)
juice of 2 limes
24 large uncooked Madagascar or tiger prawns, shelled and deveined, tails attached
coriander leaves, to garnish

limes

shelled prawns

olive oil

turmeric   *cumin*

garam masala

coriander

cayenne pepper

1 In a medium-sized bowl, whisk together well the oil, turmeric, cumin, garam masala, salt, cayenne pepper and lime juice.

2 With a small sharp knife, slit three-quarters of the way through each prawn, cutting down the centre back (be careful not to cut right through). Add the prawns to the marinade and allow to stand in a cool place for 40 minutes.

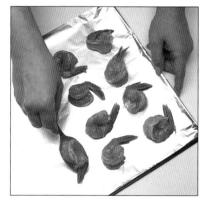

3 Preheat the grill. Arrange the prawns on a foil-lined grill pan in a single layer. Drizzle over a little of the marinade. Grill for about 2 to 3 minutes, until the prawns are glazed and curled. Serve immediately, on cocktail sticks if you like, garnished with coriander leaves.

COOK'S TIP

Wrap the prawn tails in small pieces of foil to prevent them catching and burning under the grill, then remove halfway through cooking. Make sure the prawns are cooked through and test one by cutting in half.

Caramel Cape Gooseberries

These exotic fruits resemble shiny Chinese lanterns when dipped in golden caramel. Their tartness provides a perfect contrast to the sweetness of the coating.

Makes 24

INGREDIENTS
oil, for greasing
24 Cape gooseberries
225 g/8 oz granulated sugar

Cape gooseberries

sugar

1 Lightly oil a small baking sheet. Carefully separate the papery leaves from the fruit of the Cape gooseberry and bend them back behind the berry, twisting them together at the stem.

2 Put the sugar in a small heavy saucepan, sprinkle with 30–45 ml/2–3 tbsp of water and heat over a low heat until the sugar melts, swirling the pan occasionally. Increase the heat to medium and bring to the boil. Boil for 4–5 minutes until the syrup turns a golden caramel colour.

3 Dip the base of the pan in cold water to stop the cooking, then place it in a bowl of warm water so the caramel remains liquid. Be very careful, as the caramel can cause serious burns.

4 Holding each fruit by the papery leaves, carefully dip the berry into the caramel to coat completely. Set each fruit on the prepared baking sheet and allow to cool until hard.

COCKTAILS

The true origin of the first cocktails is uncertain, but without doubt it was in America that these "mixed drinks" gained the greatest popularity and where many of the more recent cocktail bar favourites were concocted. Cocktails developed in America with bourbon, Southern Comfort and Canadian rye whisky vying for attention. Prohibition was intended to curb drinking habits but only resulted in people ingeniously distilling their own spirits, which were softened by the addition of mixers. From the late thirties and the forties the cocktail truly arrived in England. Chic and classic with a strong American twist, the Harvey Wallbanger, the Martini and the Manhattan are here to stay, but more recently, flamboyant tropical cocktails have proved popular. Coconut milk and exotic fruits are whizzed together to create long frothy cocktails. These concoctions are easily recreated at home now that exotic ingredients are readily available from large supermarkets.

Traditionally a cocktail is made from only two spirits or liqueurs and the bar person's worth is gauged by making them perfectly, with just enough zing, shaken or stirred to taste. As a general rule, the simpler cocktails and those that are served clear, are just stirred over ice, in a bar glass, before being strained into a serving glass. Drinks that contain fizzy liquids are never shaken, for the obvious, explosive reasons. Cocktails with large quantities of fruit juices, syrups or eggs are shaken over ice in a cocktail shaker; cocktails containing milk, cream, ice cream or coconut milk make wonderful, frothy drinks when whizzed in the blender.

"Bar speak" is something to get acquainted with: when a recipe suggests a dash of bitters that means just a shake of the bottle, while a squeeze of lemon rind does not mean the whole thing floating in the drink. The rind should be held over the glass and twisted in the fingers, so that the lemon oils drop into the cocktail: it is then discarded. "On the rocks" quite simply means served over ice and "straight up" means served just as it is, in a chilled glass.

At home you can create cocktails with no more than a cocktail shaker, large glass jug, blender and a few essential ingredients such as bitters, plain sugar syrup, and of course, a couple of bottles of your favourite spirits and liqueurs. Making cocktails is an enjoyable pastime, so stir up a drink, settle back and savour!

Spirits, Wines and Cider

Many cocktails contain the same spirits but in different mixes or quantities, so with a small stock of different drinks a variety of cocktails is on offer. Use the best brands available for the best results.

Brandy
Brandy is a popular spirit distilled from grape wines. There are blended brandies available from all over the world but some of the better and more expensive brandies are French. There are two main types of French brandy: cognac and armagnac. There is also a range of fruit brandies or eaux-de-vie, such as peach, cherry and apricot, as well as calvados, which is a French fruit brandy distilled from apple wine. The American equivalent is applejack. All are perfect for use in a variety of cocktails.

Champagne
Use *brut* (dry) champagne or *méthode champenoise* wines when making cocktails. You'll find that they keep their sparkle a lot longer. Some of the less expensive champagne-style supermarket wines, such as the Spanish Cava, are ideal for mixing with a variety of fruit purées, freshly squeezed fruit juices and syrups.

Cider
A drink made from fermented apple juice. Sweet or dry cider both mix well with brandy and other spirits, as does perry, a cider made with pears. Use perry in exactly the same way as apple cider to make a tasty variation.

Gin
Gin is one of our favourite spirits and is ideal for mixing with many fruit juices and liqueurs, to create some of the classic cocktails. This colourless spirit is distilled from malted barley, rye or maize. Each brand uses its own very special combination of herbs, spices and citrus oils. Juniper berries give them all their most distinctive "gin" flavour.

Ginger Wine
A golden and green wine flavoured with citrus fruits, floral scents, herbs and ginger. It is sweet but very aromatic and spicy tasting and mixes well with spirits and red wine.

Marsala
This is a delicious fortified dessert wine from Sicily. It is a blend of white wine and brandy and has a sweet caramel flavour. Most people are familiar with sweet Marsala, but are unaware that a dry version with a flavour very similar to sherry can also be bought.

Port
A full-bodied wine, fortified with brandy during fermentation. It comes from the Douro valley of Portugal and is most commonly available as tawny, ruby, white, or Late Bottled Vintage (LBV).

Rum
Distilled from sugar cane and molasses and made mostly in the West Indies, particularly Jamaica, rum is available as dark or white varieties, as well as flavoured with coconut and pineapple. It is used in cocktails such as the flamboyant Blue Hawaiian, Mai Tai and Planters Punch.

Schnapps
Generically known as aquavit, schnapps is a popular drink in Scandinavia and Germany. It is a colourless spirit made from grain starch and is also available in assorted fruit flavours such as peach, cherry, blackcurrant, pear and apple.

Sherry
This fortified wine originally came from Spain but now it is also produced in a large number of other countries such as Greece, Cyprus, South Africa and Australia. It's available in a range of styles: *fino* (pale and dry), *amontillado* (medium), *manzanilla* (medium dry), *oloroso* and *amoroso* (sweetish) and *montilla* (lower in alcohol).

Tequila
Available in clear and golden (aged) hues, tequilas are fermented and distilled in Mexico, from the juice of the agave cactus. Tequila mixed with lime juice and a little salt is Mexico's national tipple. It is also an essential ingredient in the popular Margarita where it is mixed with Cointreau and lime.

Vermouth
A high-strength wine cooked with a selection of herbs, vermouth is available as extra-dry white, bitter-sweet rosé, medium-sweet bianco and sweet red. By tradition, French vermouths are drier whilst the Italian ones tend to be sweeter.

Vodka
A colourless spirit, distilled from rye, malt or potato starch, that originated in Eastern Europe. It has a completely neutral taste, which allows it to mix well with other spirits and fruit juices. Steeping vodka with fruits, fresh herbs and spices adds flavour and interest to the cocktail.

Whisky
There are various types: Scotch whisky, Irish whiskey, the American bourbon and the Canadian rye. Whisky is distilled from either malted or unmalted grains and can also be blended.

tequila   ginger wine   dark rum   champagne   white rum   sweet vermouth   calvados

Marsala   schnapps   cognac   vodka   whisky   port   gin   fino sherry   dry vermouth

Liqueurs

Many liqueurs available today originated as medicinal tonics and a few were created by monks in their dispensaries. Liqueurs are made from a base spirit with herbs, peels of citrus fruit, spices or extracts from coffee beans.

Amaretto
A sweet Italian fruit-based liqueur with more than a hint of almonds and apricot, used in Hooded Claw and Cider Cup. It's made near the town of Saronno in Italy.

Anisette
Aniseed-flavoured liqueurs like the Italian Sambucca and the Spanish anis are often flavoured with coriander and fennel as well as aniseed. French Pernod and pastis are also anisettes, often served simply poured over plenty of ice cubes.

Bénédictine
Made from an old French recipe passed down by the Bénédictine monks of the abbey of Fécamp in Normandy, it is a golden-coloured brandy-based liqueur, flavoured with myrrh, other herbs and honey. It is an essential ingredient in the cocktail Sea Dog.

Chartreuse
A French brandy-based liqueur made from honey, herbs and spices. Originally made by Carthusian monks at La Grande Chartreuse monastery, the green liqueur has more alcohol than the yellow variety, which is flavoured with oranges and myrtle.

Cointreau
Sweet and syrupy, it is a colourless liqueur with a strong aromatic orange flavour and is often served poured over ice.

Cream Liqueurs
A mixture of cream, spirit and flavouring, such as Bailey's Irish Cream.

Crème de Cacao
A sweet liqueur originally made with cocoa beans from the Chouao region of Venezuela, it has a cocoa-vanilla flavour.

Crème de Cassis
A brandy-based blackcurrant liqueur produced in Dijon.

Crème de Menthe
A very sweet peppermint-flavoured liqueur, it also includes cinnamon, sage, ginger and orris and has strong digestive properties, which make it an ideal after-dinner drink.

Curaçao
An orange-flavoured liqueur, similar to Grand Marnier, which was originally made from the dried peel of oranges from the island of Curaçao in the West Indies. It can be blue, as used in Blue Hawaiian, white or dark orange-brown in colour.

Drambuie
A Scottish malt whisky-based liqueur, tinted with herbs, heather honey and spices. Often used in after-dinner coffee.

Galliano
A golden-coloured herb liqueur, produced in Italy, and flavoured with liquorice and aniseed.

Grand Marnier
A French curaçao, based on extracts from the bitter bergamot, orange and brandy. It is similar to triple sec, curaçao or Cointreau.

Kahlúa
A rich, brown liqueur from Mexico. Although coffee-based like Tia Maria, Kahlúa is quite different in style and is popular in the USA.

Kümmel
This caraway and fennel-flavoured liqueur is made mostly in Holland.

Southern Comfort
This American liqueur has a bourbon whiskey base and is flavoured with fruit.

Tia Maria
A Jamaican liqueur made from rum, Blue Mountain coffee extract and spices. It can be used for a less sweet version of Kahlúa.

COOK'S TIP
Make sure your cocktail cabinet is stocked up with a few of these essentials.

Southern Comfort   Kahlúa   Bénédictine   crème de menthe   Grand Marnier   Tia Maria   Drambuie

cherry brandy

Galliano

crème de cacao

Cointreau

blue curaçao

anisette

Amaretto

cream liqueur

green
Chartreuse

Mixers and Juices

Whether a cocktail is shaken or simply stirred, it is the juices and mixers that provide a drink's length and body. After all, where would the Bloody Mary be without tomato juice?

These additions to the cocktail should always be as cold as possible. Juices are best if they are made from fresh fruit but, failing that, opt for the better quality, ready-squeezed versions which are not too sweet.

Apple Juice
Available still or sparkling and either clear or cloudy. Always choose a juice with little or no extra sugar or preservatives.

Bitter Lemon
A non-alcoholic fizzy mixer – good with all white liquors. It is made from carbonated water, lemon, sugar and quinine.

Coconut Milk
Used in tropical cocktails, unsweetened coconut milk is available in cans, or in a powdered form. The powder requires dissolving in hot water and then should be left to cool.

Cranberry Juice
A tangy and refreshing fruit drink, available in cartons and glass jars. The regular cranberry juice mixes well with spirits; other cranberry juices, mixed with raspberry or apple juice, offer further delicious flavor combinations.

Ginger Ale
Available in several varieties: dry, Canadian dry and the slightly

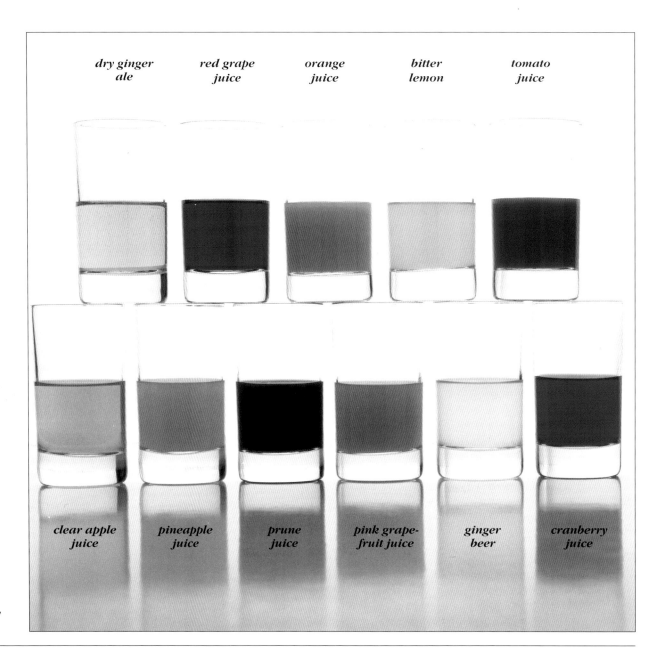

dry ginger ale   *red grape juice*   *orange juice*   *bitter lemon*   *tomato juice*

clear apple juice   *pineapple juice*   *prune juice*   *pink grape-fruit juice*   *ginger beer*   *cranberry juice*

Ginger Ale
Available in several varieties: dry, Canadian dry and the slightly sweeter American dry. A non-alcoholic mixer, it is made from carbonated water, ginger extract and sugar. Mixes well with whisky, bourbon and gin and is used in Kew Pimms.

Ginger Beer
A fermented drink made from ginger, sugar, water and yeast. The alcohol content in ginger beer is negligible.

Lemonade
Usually a non-alcoholic fizzy soft drink. Alcoholic and some traditional lemonade varieties are now available.

Orange Juice
For best results, either squeeze fresh oranges yourself or purchase chilled orange juice made from 100% fresh fruit. These have nothing added and certainly no extra sugar. Other orange juices are mostly made with sweetened concentrates.

Passion-fruit Cordial and Nectar
These are made with concentrated passion-fruit juice and natural flavourings. The cordial is very strong and needs diluting, to taste.

Pineapple Juice
The sweet and sour flavour of pineapple juice is imperative in many tropical cocktails. Use either freshly-squeezed or cartons, but preferably use the less sweet varieties.

Pink Grapefruit Juice
Often made from Florida pink grapefruit which are naturally

sweet, it mixes well with white spirits. Look out for juices made from freshly squeezed fruit.

Prune Juice
This is imported from America and is made from a concentrate of dried prunes with no added sugar or preservatives.

Red Grape Juice
A light and fruity juice which is useful for making non-alcoholic cocktails. Choose cartons to keep in the cupboard and once opened, store in the fridge for up to three days.

Soda Water
A mixer containing sparkling water and bicarbonate of soda. Traditionally mixed with whisky and good to use when making long thirst-quenching cocktails. Sparkling mineral water can be used in its place.

Tomato Juice
An excellent versatile mixer available in thick or thin consistencies. It can be found, mixed with clam juice, in a Canadian product called Clamato.

Tonic Water
A good old-fashioned mixer which is used with gin, vodka or whisky. Available in a low calorie variety. It contains a small amount of quinine.

Added Flavours

These are the little extras that make all the difference between a good or a boring cocktail.

Bitters, Syrups and Sauces
The most widely used is angostura bitters, made in the West Indies from cloves, cinnamon, gentian, mace, nutmeg, quinine, prunes and other barks, stems and herbs. It has a distinctive flavour and rosy-red hue when a few drops are used. Grenadine and lime cordial both add sweetness and hints of their own individual flavours of pomegranate and lime. Grenadine is also used for its pink/red colour which creates a glowing band at the bottom of a Mai-Tai and a Tequila Sunrise.
   Other herbs and spices are vital for their flavours and are used in making Tabasco sauce and Worcestershire sauce, both of which are used for maximum impact in a Bloody Mary. Balsamic and cider vinegars add a tart flavour but are less sour than lemon or lime juice.

Herbs
Ground celery seeds, fresh mint or lemon balm leaves and, during the summer months, fresh borage, chive or thyme flowers add hints of aromatic flavours. These are used to great effect for their individual tastes and also for added colour and decoration.

Spices
Freshly-grated nutmeg, cloves, bruised cardamom pods, sticks of cinnamon and a pinch of cayenne, all pep up a basic

punch or egg-nog; and freshly-grated or creamed horseradish and fresh ginger add a zing all of their own to the simplest of juices. Use any spice with care, since an over-eager hand can easily upset the delicate balance of a cocktail. Taste as you go along and then add a little more if liked.

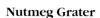

Cocktail Equipment

To make a successful cocktail you need a few essential pieces of barman's equipment. The most vital and flamboyant is the cocktail shaker; what you have in the cupboard can usually be substituted for the rest. The equipment is listed below in descending order of importance.

Cocktail Shaker
A cocktail shaker is used for those cocktails made with juices and syrups that need good mixing but do not depend upon being crystal clear. Shakers are made of stainless steel, silver, perspex or tough glass. The Boston shaker is made of two cup-type containers that fit over each other, one normally made of glass, the other of metal. This type is often preferred by professional bar staff. For beginners the classic three-piece shaker is easier to handle, with its base to hold the ice and liquids, a top fitted with a built-in strainer and a tight-fitting cap.

Blender
Goblet blenders are the best shape for mixing cocktails that need to be aerated, to create a frothy cocktail, or to be blended with finely crushed ice. A word of warning: do not be tempted to crush the ice in the blender, since this will blunt the blade. Opt for a tea towel or cloth bag and a rolling pin and save your blender from ruin.

Ice Bag or Cloth
Essential for holding ice cubes when crushing, either to roughly cracked lumps or to fine snow. Both the ice bag and cloth must be scrupulously clean.

Wooden Hammer
For crushing the ice, the end of a wooden rolling pin will also work well.

Tot Measures or Measuring Jug
For measuring out the required quantities. The measurements can be in single (22.5 ml) or double (45 ml) bar measures, fluid ounces or millilitres. Do not switch from one type of measurement to another.
1 measure equals 22.5 ml/ 1 1/2 tbsp.

Strainer
Used when pouring drinks from shaker or bar glass to cocktail glass, the best strainers are made from stainless steel and look like a flat spoon, with holes and with a curl of wire on the underside. These are held over the top of the glass to hold the fruit and ice back.

Mixing Jug or Bar Glass
It is useful to have a container in which to mix and stir drinks that are not shaken. The glass or jug should be large enough to hold two or three drinks. This method is intended for drinks that are meant to be clear, not cloudy.

Corkscrew
For the obvious reasons. The fold away type, with a can opener and

bottle-top opener, is very useful to have to hand for all drink-opening possibilities.

Bar Spoon
These long-handled spoons can reach to the bottom of the tallest tumblers and are used for mixing the drink directly in the glass. Some have a disc base at the top.

Muddler
A long stick with a bulbous end, which is used for crushing sugar or mint leaves, and so is particularly useful when creating juleps. There are a variety of sizes. They are either used like a pestle in a bar glass, or, in a smaller version, in the individual glass.

Lemon Knife and Squeezer
Citrus fruit are vital in many cocktails; a good quality sharp knife is required for cutting fruit and the squeezer for extracting juice. Fruit juice presses are quicker to use but more costly.

Nutmeg Grater
A tiny grater with small holes, for grating this hard nut over egg-nogs and frothy drinks.

Straws, Swizzle and Cocktail Sticks
Used for the finishing decorative touches that complete a cocktail.

Zester and Canelle Knife
For presenting fruit when dressing glasses. If you do not already have these, do not run out and buy them, since drinks can look equally attractive with more simply sliced fruit.

Right: *1: blender; 2: cocktail shakers; 3: fruit juice press; 4: wooden hammer; 5: canelle knife; 6: corkscrew; 7: bar spoon; 8: strainer; 9: drinking straws; 10: tot measures; 11: measuring spoons; 12: cup measures; 13: cocktail sticks; 14: swizzle sticks; 15: nutmeg grater; 16: cloth; 17: sharp knife.*

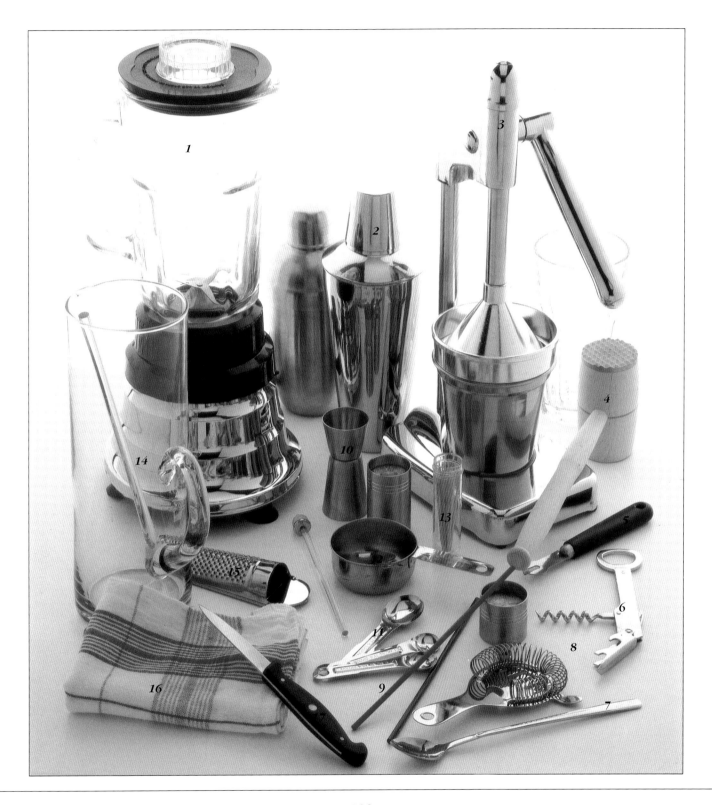

Glasses

Glasses should always be washed and dried with a glass cloth to ensure they are sparkling clean. Although some recipes suggest chilled glasses, don't be tempted to put the best crystal in the freezer; leave it at the back of the fridge instead.

Cocktail or Martini Glasses
Classic and elegant, this glass is a wide conical bowl on a tall stem, which keeps warm hands away from the drink. It holds about 150 ml/¼ pint.

Collins Glass
The tallest of the tumblers, narrow with perfectly straight sides, it holds about 300 ml/½ pint and is typically used for long drinks made with fresh juices or topped up with soda.

Old-fashioned Glass
Classic shorts (whisky) tumblers are used for shorter drinks, which are served "on the rocks". They hold about 175 ml/6 fl oz.

Highball Glass
The middle-sized tumbler and the most used. It holds about 250 ml/8 fl oz.

Liqueur Glass
A tiny glass for small measures of about 50 ml/2 fl oz.

Brandy Balloon or Snifter
This glass has been designed to trap the fragrance of the brandy in the bowl of the glass. The cocktail is further helped by being cupped in the palms of the hands to warm it gently and release the aromas.

Large Cocktail Goblets
These vary in size and shape and are used for serving larger frothy drinks, such as tropical cocktails and Piña Coladas. The wider rims of these glasses leave plenty of room for flamboyant decoration.

Champagne Glasses
Champagne can be poured either into attractive and old-fashioned champagne bowls or tall and slim flutes. The champagne flute is the more acceptable glass to use as it is more efficient at conserving the fizz and the bubbles.

Red Wine Balloon
The most useful size of wine glass, holding 300 ml/½ pint. They are only filled to half their capacity to allow the wine to be swirled around inside.

White Wine Glass
This is a long-stemmed medium-sized glass that, once again, keeps warm hands away from the chilled wine or cocktail.

Pousse-café
A thin and narrow glass standing on a short stem. Used for floating or layered stronger liqueur cocktails.

Above: *1: cocktail glass; 2: Collins glass; 3: old-fashioned glass; 4: highball glass; 5: liqueur glass; 6: brandy balloon; 7: large cocktail goblet; 8: champagne flute; 9: champagne bowl; 10: red wine balloon; 11: white wine glass; 12: pousse-café.*

Garnishes

It is far more eye-catching not to over-dress cocktails, otherwise they all too quickly look like a fruit salad. Less is best! These little extra edible garnishes should reflect the contents of the glass.

Frosting glasses with salt and sugar is a simple but effective touch, which hardly needs much extra help or assistance.

Edible garnishes are always best and should reflect the contents of the cocktail. Citrus fruit are widely used because they stay appetizing to look at and can be cut in advance and kept covered in the fridge, for a day, until required. Apple, pear and banana are suitable, but they do discolour on exposure to the air; dip them in lemon juice first.

Soft fruit such as strawberries, fresh cherries, peaches, apricots and redcurrants make fabulous splashes of colour and add a delicious flavour, but are only available during the summer.

The maraschino cherry is a popular option and the never ending supply of exotic fruits available all year round, such as mango, pineapple and star fruit together offer endless decorative possibilities.

But not all garnishes and decorations are fruit-based. Grated chocolate and nutmeg adorn egg-nogs and flips, while some Martinis call for a green olive – always opt for those in brine and not in oil. Plain or steeped-chilli vodka can stand pickled chillies and the Gibson (a dry Martini cocktail) couldn't be a Gibson without a white pearl onion to complete it.

Crushing Ice

Some cocktails require cracked or crushed ice for adding to glasses, or a finely crushed ice snow for blending. It is not a good idea to do this in a blender or food processor as you may find it makes the blade blunt.

Making Decorative Ice Cubes

Decorative ice cubes can instantly jazz up simple cocktails. Flavour and colour ice cubes with fruit juices or bitters and freeze as normal.

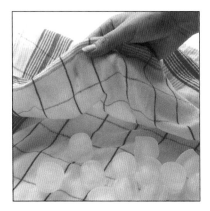

1 Lay a cloth on a work surface and cover half of the cloth with ice cubes. Alternatively, place the ice cubes in a cloth ice bag.

2 Fold the cloth over and, using the end of a rolling pin or a wooden mallet, strike the ice firmly, several times, until you achieve the required fineness.

1 Fill each compartment of an ice cube tray half-full with water and place in the freezer for 2–3 hours or until the water has frozen.

2 Prepare the fruit, olives, mint leaves, lemon rind, raisins or borage flowers and dip each briefly in water. Place in the ice-cube trays and freeze again.

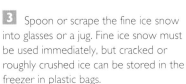

3 Spoon or scrape the fine ice snow into glasses or a jug. Fine ice snow must be used immediately, but cracked or roughly crushed ice can be stored in the freezer in plastic bags.

3 Top up the ice cube trays with water and return to the freezer to freeze completely. Use as required.

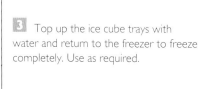

Frosting Glasses

Frosting adds both to the look and the taste of a cocktail. Use celery salt, grated coconut, grated chocolate, coloured sugars or cocoa for a similar effect. Once frosted, place the glass in the fridge to chill, until needed.

Shaking Cocktails

Cocktails that contain sugar syrups or creams require more than just a stir and are combined and chilled by briefly shaking together with ice. Remember that it is only possible to shake one or two servings at a time.

1 Hold the glass upside-down, so the juice does not run down the glass. Rub the rim of the glass with the cut surface of a lemon, lime, orange or even a slice of fresh pineapple.

2 Keeping the glass upside-down, dip the rim into a shallow layer of sugar or salt. Re-dip the glass, if necessary, so the rim is well-coated.

1 Fill the cocktail shaker two-thirds full with ice cubes and pour in the spirits; add the mixers, if not sparkling, and the flavouring ingredients.

2 Put the lid on the shaker. Hold the shaker firmly, keeping the lid in place with one hand.

3 Stand the glass upright and leave it until the salt and sugar has dried on the rim, then chill.

3 Shake vigorously, for about 10 seconds to blend simple concoctions and for 20–30 seconds for drinks with sugar syrups or eggs. By this time the outside of the shaker should feel chilled.

4 Remove the small lid and pour into the prepared glass, using a strainer if the shaker is not already fitted with one.

Making Basic Sugar Syrup

A sugar syrup is sometimes preferable to crystal sugars for sweetening cocktails, since it immediately blends with the other ingredients.

Makes about 750 ml/24 fl oz

INGREDIENTS
350 g/12 oz caster sugar
600 ml/20 fl oz water

1 Place the sugar in a heavy-based pan with the water, and heat gently over a low heat. Stir with a wooden spoon until the sugar has dissolved.

2 Brush the sides of the pan with a pastry brush dampened in water to remove any sugar crystals that might cause the sugar syrup to crystallize.

3 Bring to the boil for 3–5 minutes. Skim off any scum and, when no more appears, remove the pan from the heat.

4 Cool and pour into clean, dry, airtight bottles. Keep in the fridge for up to one month.

Making Flavoured Syrups

Syrup can be flavoured with any ingredient you like. Add to the basic syrup, bring to the boil, then bottle with the syrup.

Makes about 450 ml/15 fl oz

INGREDIENTS
900 g/2 lb very ripe soft or stone fruit, washed
350 g/12 oz caster sugar

COOK'S TIP
Raspberries, black or redcurrants, plums and peaches all make delicious flavoured syrups.

1 Place the washed fruit of your choice in a bowl and, using the bottom of a rolling pin, a wooden pestle or a potato masher, crush the fruit to release the juices. Cover and leave overnight to concentrate the flavour.

2 Strain the purée through a cloth bag or piece of muslin. Gather the corners of the cloth together and twist them tightly to remove as much juice as possible. Measure the amount of juice and add 225 g/8 oz sugar to every 300 ml/½ pint fruit juice.

3 Place the pan over a low heat and gently stir until all the sugar has dissolved. Continue as in the recipe for basic sugar syrup. The syrup will keep in the fridge for up to one month.

Making Flavoured Spirits

Gin, vodka and white rum can be left to steep and absorb the flavours of a wide variety of soft fruits.

Makes 1.2 litre/40 fl oz

INGREDIENTS
450 g/1 lb raspberries,
  strawberries, pineapple or sloes
225 g/8 oz caster sugar
1 litre/35 fl oz gin or vodka

VARIATIONS
Vodka and sliced bananas;
white rum and fresh pineapple;
gin and drained, canned lychees;
sliced peaches or apricots; brandy
and plums or apricots.

1 Place the fruit in a wide-necked jar and add the sugar. If using sloes, prick them with a needle or fine skewer, to release their flavour.

2 Add the spirit. Cover tightly. Leave in a cool, dark place for a month, shaking gently every week.

3 Strain through muslin or a cloth bag and squeeze out the rest of the liquid from the steeped fruit.

4 Return the flavoured spirit to a clean bottle, seal and store it in a cool, dark place.

Steeping Spirits

Steeping any spirit with a strong flavouring ingredient, such as chillies, creates an interestingly flavoured spirit.

Makes 1 litre/35 fl oz

INGREDIENTS
1 litre/35 fl oz sherry or vodka
25–50 g/1–2 oz small red chillies,
  or to taste

1 Wash and dry the chillies, discarding any chillies that are less than perfect. Using a cocktail stick, prick the chillies all over to release their flavours.

2 Pack the chillies tightly into a sterilized bottle.

3 Top up with sherry or vodka. Fit the cork tightly and leave in a dark place for at least ten days or up to two months.

VARIATIONS
Try the following interesting alternatives: gin with cumin seeds, star anise or juniper berries; brandy with 25 g/1 oz peeled and sliced fresh root ginger or 15 g/$\frac{1}{2}$ oz whole cloves; vodka with 50 g/2 oz washed raisins or 1–2 tbsp cracked black peppercorns; rum with 2–3 pricked vanilla pods. The amount of flavouring used is a question of personal taste.

Gin Smash

This simple and very refreshing cocktail can be made with fresh peppermint, apple mint or black mint to produce three uniquely flavoured drinks. Use the variety of mint you prefer.

VARIATION
Use Southern Comfort or bourbon in place of the gin.

Serves 1

INGREDIENTS
15 ml/1 tbsp caster sugar
4 fresh sprigs of mint
2 measures/45 ml/3 tbsp dry gin

gin

caster sugar

mint

1 Dissolve the sugar in a little water in the cocktail shaker.

2 Place some ice cubes in a clean tea towel and crush them finely.

3 Add the mint to the cocktail shaker and, using a muddler, bruise and press the juices out of the mint.

4 Half-fill the shaker with the cracked ice and add the gin.

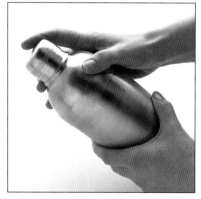

5 Put on the top and shake the cocktail for about 20 seconds, to mix the gin with the mint.

6 Strain the cocktail into a small wine glass filled with crushed ice. If liked, add fresh mint sprigs and drinking straws.

Gall Bracer

Short and smart, this drink is served on the rocks, in a tumbler for a man or in a delicate long-stemmed cocktail glass, with a maraschino cherry, for a lady.

Serves 1

INGREDIENTS
2 dashes angostura bitters
2 dashes grenadine
2 measures/45 ml/3 tbsp whisky
lemon rind
maraschino cherry, to decorate
  (optional)

grenadine

maraschino cherry

whisky

angostura bitters

1 Half-fill a bar glass with ice. Add the angostura bitters, grenadine and whisky and stir well to chill.

2 Place some ice in a short tumbler and pour the cocktail over it.

3 Holding the lemon rind between the fingers, squeeze out the oils and juices into the cocktail. Discard the lemon rind.

4 Add a cherry, if you like.

VARIATION

For a longer drink, top up with soda or sparkling mineral water, or for a cocktail called a Gall Trembler substitute gin for the whisky and add more bitters.

Gibson

Well loved in Japan, this is a version of the Martini with a small white onion in it, rather than the twist of lemon. You may prefer a higher proportion of gin.

Serves 1

INGREDIENTS
1/2 measure/10 ml/2 tsp extra-dry
   vermouth
1 scant measure/20 ml/1 1/4 tbsp
   extra-dry gin
2 pearl onions, to decorate

extra-dry vermouth

gin

pearl onions

VARIATION

Add a touch more dry vermouth and a twist of lemon and you have an Australian Kangaroo.

1 Pour the vermouth into a bar glass of ice, stir briskly and then pour out. Only the vermouth that clings to the ice and glass should be used.

2 Add the gin and stir for at least 30 seconds, to chill well.

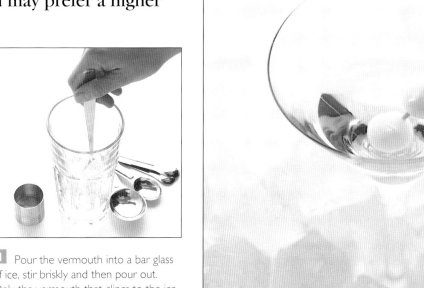

3 Strain into a martini glass either on the rocks or straight up.

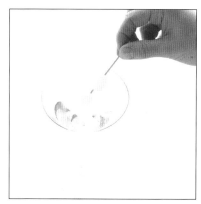

4 Thread the pearl onions on to a cocktail stick and add to the drink.

Brandy Alexander

A warming digestif, made from a blend of crème de cacao, brandy and double cream, that can be served at the end of the meal with coffee.

Serves 1

INGREDIENTS
1 measure/22.5 ml/1½ tbsp
  brandy
1 measure/22.5 ml/1½ tbsp
  crème de cacao
1 measure/22.5 ml/1½ tbsp
  double cream
whole nutmeg, grated,
  to decorate

crème de cacao

nutmeg

double cream

brandy

1 Half-fill the cocktail shaker with ice and pour in the brandy, crème de cacao and, finally, the cream.

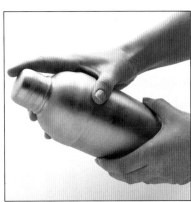

2 Shake for about 20 seconds, to mix together well.

3 Strain the chilled cocktail into a small wine glass.

4 Finely grate a little nutmeg over the top of the cocktail.

VARIATION

Warm the brandy and the double cream gently and add to a blender with the crème de cacao. Whizz until frothy. Serve with a cinnamon stick.

Perfect Manhattan

When making Manhattans it's a matter of preference whether you use sweet vermouth, dry vermouth or a mixture. Both of the former require a dash of angostura bitters.

Serves 1

INGREDIENTS
2 measures/45 ml/3 tbsp rye
    whisky
¹/₄ measure/5 ml/1 tsp dry
    French vermouth
¹/₄ measure/5 ml/1 tsp sweet
    Italian vermouth
lemon rind and a maraschino
    cherry, to decorate

sweet vermouth

maraschino cherry

whisky

dry vermouth

lemon rind

VARIATION

Create a Skyscraper by adding a dash of angostura bitters, a teaspoon of maraschino cherry juice, and top up with ginger ale.

1 Pour the whisky and vermouths into a bar glass of ice. Stir well for about 30 seconds, to mix and chill.

2 Strain, on the rocks or straight up, into a chilled cocktail glass.

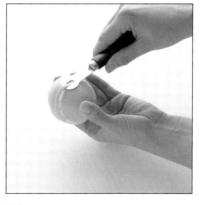

3 Using a canelle knife, pare away a small strip of lemon rind. Tie it into a knot, to help release the oils from the rind, and drop it into the cocktail.

4 To finish, add a maraschino cherry with its stalk left intact.

Margarita

Traditionally this popular strong apéritif is made with tequila and Cointreau, but it is also good made with vodka and triple sec (a term used for white curaçao).

VARIATION

Replace the Cointreau with blue curaçao for an interesting colour and flavour.

Serves 1

INGREDIENTS
1 measure/22.5 ml/1½ tbsp tequila
1 measure/22.5 ml/1½ tbsp Cointreau
⅔ measure/15 ml/1 tbsp lime juice
wedge of fresh lime, fine salt crystals, and cucumber peel, to decorate

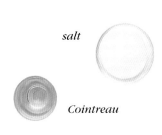

tequila

salt

Cointreau

lime juice

cucumber peel

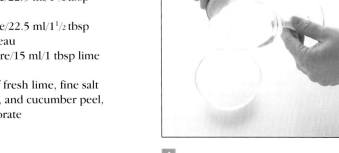

1 Rub the rim of the glass with a wedge of fresh lime.

2 Invert the glass into fine salt, to create a rim of salt. Turn the glass the right way up and chill until required.

3 Pour the tequila and Cointreau, with the lime juice, into a cocktail shaker filled with ice. Shake for 20 seconds.

4 Carefully strain the cocktail into the frosted glass.

5 Using a sharp knife or vegetable peeler, cut a long thin strip of green peel from a whole cucumber.

6 Trim the cucumber peel to size and thread it on to a cocktail stick. Add to the glass to decorate.

Hooded Claw

Syrupy-sweet prune juice with Amaretto and Cointreau makes a delicious digestif when poured over finely crushed ice snow.

Serves 4

INGREDIENTS
5 measures/120 ml/4 fl oz prune juice
2 measures/45 ml/3 tbsp Amaretto
1 measure/22.5 ml/1¹/₂ tbsp Cointreau

Amaretto

Cointreau

prune juice

1 Pour the prune juice, Amaretto and Cointreau together into a cocktail shaker half-filled with ice.

2 Shake the cocktail for 20 seconds, to chill well.

VARIATION
Mix 6 parts prune juice with 1 part elderflower cordial, for a tangy, non-alcoholic version. Serve it on the rocks and super-cold.

3 Loosely fill four small liqueur glasses with finely crushed ice snow.

4 Strain the drink into the glasses and serve with short drinking straws.

Bitter Gimlet

An old-fashioned apéritif, which could easily be turned into a longer drink by topping up with chilled tonic or soda water.

Serves 1

INGREDIENTS
1 lime, cut into wedges
1 measure/22.5 ml/1½ tbsp gin
2 dashes angostura bitters
slice and rind of lime, to decorate

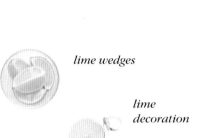

lime wedges

lime decoration

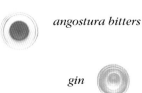

angostura bitters

gin

VARIATION

Add a teaspoon of sugar, for a sweeter version, or add a dash or two of crème de menthe to create a Fallen Angel.

1 Place the lime at the bottom of the bar glass and, using a muddler, press the juice out of the lime.

2 Add cracked ice, the gin and the bitters and stir well, until cold.

3 Strain the cocktail into a short tumbler over ice cubes.

4 Add a triangle of lime rind to the drink and use a slice of lime to decorate the rim of the glass.

Chilli Vodkatini

Not quite a Martini, but almost. Over the years the proportions of spirit to vermouth have varied widely, with the vodka becoming almost overwhelming. Be sure to have your chilli vodka made well in advance and ready to use.

VARIATION
For the classic Martini, use gin, but serve with a twist of lemon. Mix plain vodka and dry vermouth for a Vodka Martini. Add an olive and it becomes a Vodka Gibson.

Serves 1

INGREDIENTS
1 measure/22.5 ml/1½ tbsp chilli
   vodka
¼ measure/5 ml/1 tsp medium or
   dry French vermouth
2 small pickled or vodka-soaked
   chillies, to decorate
1 pitted green olive, to decorate

chilli vodka

dry vermouth

chilli-stuffed olive

1 Add the chilli vodka to a bar glass of ice and mix for about 30 seconds, until the outside of the glass has frosted.

2 Add the vermouth to a chilled cocktail glass and swirl it round the inside of the glass, to moisten it. Discard any remaining vermouth.

3 Cut one of the pickled chillies in half and discard the seeds. Stuff the pitted green olive with the chilli.

4 Thread the stuffed olive on to a cocktail stick, together with the remaining chilli.

5 Strain the cocktail into the prepared cocktail glass.

6 Add the olive and chilli decoration to the drink before serving.

Gin Crusta

Prepare the glass in advance and keep it chilled in the fridge ready for instant use! The depth of pink colour will depend on the strength of the maraschino cherry juice.

VARIATION
Make in the same way with whisky, Southern Comfort, brandy or rum.

Serves 1

INGREDIENTS
1 lemon
30 ml/2 tbsp golden granulated
  sugar
3 dashes sugar syrup
2 dashes maraschino cherry juice
2 dashes angostura bitters
1 measure/22.5 ml/1½ tbsp dry
  gin

 angostura bitters

maraschino cherry juice

 golden granulated sugar

 lemon juice

 gin

 sugar syrup

 lemon rind

1 Cut both ends off the lemon and, using a sharp knife or canelle knife, peel the lemon thinly, as you would an apple, in one long continuous piece.

2 Halve the whole lemon and rub the edge of a glass with one half.

3 Turn the glass upside-down and dip it into the granulated sugar, to create a decorative rim.

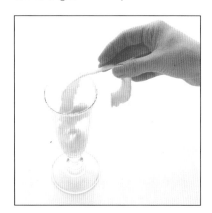

4 Arrange the lemon rind in a scroll on the inside of the glass.

5 Place the sugar syrup, maraschino cherry juice, angostura bitters, gin and juice of ¼ of the lemon in a cocktail shaker, half-filled with ice.

6 Shake for about 30 seconds and carefully strain into the prepared glass.

Airstrike

A variation on a Val d'Isère Shooter, similar in idea to the Italian Flaming Sambucca.

Serves 1

INGREDIENTS
2 measures/45 ml/3 tbsp Galliano
1 measure/22.5 ml/1½ tbsp
    brandy
1 star anise

Galliano

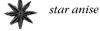

star anise

brandy

VARIATION

Use all Sambucca and float two or three coffee beans on the surface instead of the star anise before lighting.

1 Put the Galliano and brandy in a small saucepan and heat very gently, until just warm.

2 Carefully pour into a heat-resistant glass standing on a small plate or saucer; add the star anise.

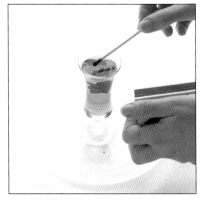

4 Leave to burn for a couple of minutes, until the star anise has sizzled a little and released extra aroma into the drink. Leave to cool slightly before drinking. The top of the glass will be hot!

3 Using a lighted taper or long match, pass the flame over the surface of the drink to ignite it. The flame will be low and very pale, so be careful not to burn yourself.

B52

This cocktail depends on the difference in specific weight or densities of each of the liqueurs to remain strictly separated in layers.

Serves 1

INGREDIENTS
1 measure/22.5 ml/1¹/₂ tbsp
    Kahlúa
1 measure/22.5 ml/1¹/₂ tbsp
    Grand Marnier
1 measure/22.5 ml/1¹/₂ tbsp
    Bailey's Irish Cream

Grand Marnier

Bailey's Irish Cream

Kahlúa

VARIATION

Create a similar layered effect with equal quantities of Bailey's, Kahlúa and vodka, layered in that order. Or try Chartreuse, cherry brandy and kümmel, with cumin seeds floated on the top.

1 In a small shooter or pousse-café glass, pour a 2 cm/³/₄ in layer of Kahlúa.

2 Hold a cold teaspoon upside-down, only just touching the surface of the Kahlúa and the side of the glass.

3 Slowly and carefully pour the Grand Marnier over the back of the teaspoon, to create a second layer.

4 In the same way, carefully pour the Bailey's over the back of a second clean teaspoon, to create a final layer. This layer in fact will form the middle layer and push the Grand Marnier to the top!

Coffee and Chocolate Flip

Since the egg is not cooked, use only the freshest eggs. Drambuie can be used instead of brandy for a hint of honey, but don't add the sugar. Substitute Tia Maria for the Kahlúa, for a less sweet version.

VARIATION
Shake together equal quantities of Kahlúa, chocolate-flavoured milk and coffee. Serve on the rocks.

Serves 1

INGREDIENTS
1 egg
1 tsp caster sugar
1 measure/22.5 ml/1½ tbsp brandy
1 measure/22.5 ml/1½ tbsp Kahlúa
5 ml/1 tsp instant coffee granules
3 measures/70 ml/4½ tbsp double cream
drinking chocolate powder or grated chocolate, to decorate

instant coffee granules

egg

caster sugar

drinking chocolate powder

double cream   *Kahlúa*

brandy

1 Separate the egg and lightly beat the egg white until frothy and white.

2 In a separate bowl or glass, beat the egg yolk with the sugar.

3 In a small saucepan, gently warm together the brandy, Kahlúa, coffee granules and cream.

4 Whisk the cooled cream mixture into the egg yolk.

5 Add the egg white to the egg and cream and pour the mixture briefly back and forth between two glasses, until the mixture is smooth.

6 Pour into a tall glass over coarsely crushed ice and sprinkle the top with drinking chocolate powder.

Cranberry Kiss

A delicious full-flavoured cocktail, with the tang of cranberry and pink grapefruit juices and the sweetness of Marsala.

VARIATION

Shake together cranberry and pineapple juice with coconut milk. Add vodka or gin to taste.

Serves 1

INGREDIENTS

2 measures/45 ml/3 tbsp cranberry juice
1 measure/22.5 ml/1½ tbsp brandy
2 measures/45 ml/3 tbsp pink grapefruit juice
2 measures/45 ml/3 tbsp Marsala
redcurrant string, to decorate
1 egg white, lightly beaten, to decorate
15 g/½ oz caster sugar, to decorate

1 Lightly brush the redcurrants with the egg white.

2 Shake caster sugar over the redcurrants, to cover them in a light frosting. Leave aside to dry.

3 Place the cranberry juice with the brandy and grapefruit juice in a cocktail shaker full of crushed ice and shake for 20 seconds to mix.

caster sugar

egg white

brandy

cranberry juice

pink grapefruit juice

Marsala

redcurrant string

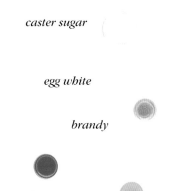

4 Strain into a well-chilled glass.

5 Tilt the glass slightly, before slowly pouring the Marsala into the drink down the side of the glass.

6 Serve decorated with the frosted redcurrant string.

Grasshopper

A minted, creamy cocktail in an attractive shade of green. If you use dark crème de cacao the cocktail will not be as vibrant a green colour but you'll find that it will taste just as good.

Serves 1

INGREDIENTS
2 measures/45 ml/3 tbsp crème de menthe
2 measures/45 ml/3 tbsp light crème de cacao
2 measures/45 ml/3 tbsp double cream
melted plain chocolate, to decorate

double cream

crème de menthe

crème de cacao

plain chocolate

VARIATION

Process in a blender, with crushed ice, for a smoother consistency. For a Scandinavian Freeze, mix vodka with crème de cacao and a scoop of vanilla ice cream and process just until smooth.

1 Measure the crème de menthe and crème de cacao into a cocktail shaker and add the cream.

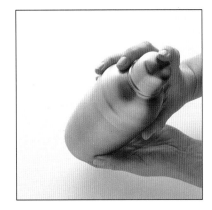

2 Add some cracked ice and shake well for 20 seconds.

3 Strain the cocktail into a tumbler of finely-cracked ice.

4 To decorate, spread the melted chocolate evenly over a plastic board and leave to cool and harden. Using a sharp knife draw the blade across the chocolate to create curls. Add to the top of the cocktail and serve.

Tequila Sunset

A variation on the popular party drink which can be mixed and chilled in a jug, ready to pour into glasses, and finished off at the last minute with the addition of crème de cassis and honey.

Serves 1

INGREDIENTS

1 measure/22.5 ml/1^{1}/$_{2}$ tbsp clear
   or golden tequila
5 measures/120 ml/ 4 fl oz lemon
   juice, chilled
1 measure/22.5 ml/1^{1}/$_{2}$ tbsp
   orange juice, chilled
10–30 ml/1–2 tbsp clear honey
^{2}/$_{3}$ measure/15 ml/1 tbsp crème
   de cassis

crème de cassis

lemon juice

tequila

clear honey

orange juice

1 Pour the tequila and then the lemon and orange juices straight into a well-chilled cocktail glass.

2 Using a swizzle stick, mix the ingredients by twisting the stick between the palms of your hands.

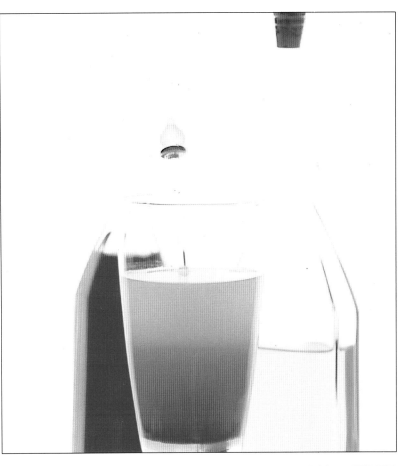

3 Drizzle the honey into the centre of the cocktail and it will fall and create a layer at the bottom of the glass.

4 Add the crème de cassis, but do not stir. It will create a glowing layer above the honey at the bottom of the glass.

VARIATION

To make a Tequila Sunrise, mix 2 parts tequila with 6 parts orange juice and 2 parts grenadine and stir gently together.

Vunderful

A long, lazy Sunday afternoon tipple, conjured up in the heat of Zimbabwe. Leave the fruits in the gin for as long as possible.

VARIATION
Use fresh apricots or nectarines and top up with either ginger beer or ginger ale.

Serves 20

INGREDIENTS
400 g/14 oz can lychees
2 peaches, sliced
600 ml/20 fl oz gin

For each person you will need:
1 measure/22.5 ml/1½ tbsp Pimms
2–3 dashes angostura bitters
5 measures/120 ml/4 fl oz chilled
    tonic water or lemonade
slices of lime, to decorate

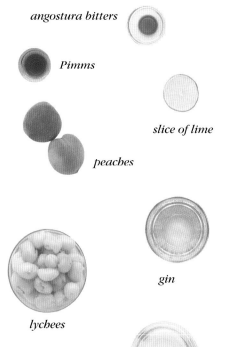

angostura bitters

Pimms

slice of lime

peaches

gin

lychees

lemonade

1 Strain the lychees from the syrup and place them in a wide-necked jar with the peach slices and the gin. Leave overnight or for up to a month.

2 Mix for each person, in a large bar glass or jug, 1 measure/22.5ml/1½ tbsp lychee gin with 1 measure/22.5 ml/1½ tbsp Pimms and add bitters to taste.

3 Strain into tall tumblers filled with ice cubes.

4 Add chilled tonic water or lemonade, to taste.

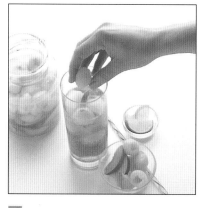

5 Put some of the drained gin-soaked lychees and peaches into each glass and add a muddler, with which to stir and crush the fruit into the drink.

6 Add a half slice of lime to the rim of the glass and serve.

Blue Hawaiian

This drink can be decorated as flamboyantly as Carmen Miranda's head-dress with a mixture of fruits and leaves. An eye-catching colour, but you'll find it very drinkable.

Serves 1

INGREDIENTS
1 measure/22.5 ml/1½ tbsp blue curaçao
1 measure/22.5 ml/1½ tbsp coconut cream
2 measures/45 ml/3 tbsp white rum
2 measures/45 ml/3 tbsp pineapple juice

TO DECORATE:
leaves and wedge of pineapple
slice of prickly pear
wedge of lime
maraschino cherry

pineapple juice

white rum

prickly pear

lime wedge

maraschino cherry

pineapple wedge

pineapple leaves

blue curaçao

coconut cream

VARIATION
Pour equal quantities of vodka and blue curaçao over ice. Top up with lemonade for a Blue Lagoon or add equal quantities of gin and curaçao, plus angostura bitters, for a Blue Cloak.

1 Put the curacao, coconut cream and white rum in a blender. Process very briefly until the colour is even.

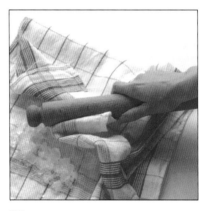

2 Place ice cubes between a tea towel and crush to a fine snow with a wooden hammer or rolling pin.

3 Add the pineapple juice to the blender and process the mixture once more, until frothy.

4 Spoon the crushed ice into a large cocktail glass or goblet.

5 Pour the cocktail from the blender over the crushed ice.

6 Decorate with the pineapple leaves and wedge, prickly pear slices, a lime wedge and a maraschino cherry. Serve with a couple of drinking straws.

Mai Tai

A very refreshing, but strong, party drink that slips down easily; just before you do!

Serves 1

INGREDIENTS
1 measure/22.5 ml/1¹/₂ tbsp
    white rum
1 measure/22.5 ml/1¹/₂ tbsp dark
    rum
1 measure/22.5 ml/1¹/₂ tbsp
    apricot brandy
3 measures/70 ml/4¹/₂ tbsp
    orange juice, chilled
3 measures/70 ml/4¹/₂ tbsp
    pineapple juice, chilled
1 measure/22.5 ml/1¹/₂ tbsp
    grenadine

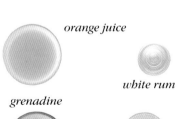
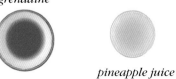
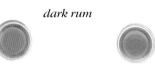

orange juice

white rum

grenadine

pineapple juice

dark rum

apricot brandy

VARIATION
Mix bitters, rum, orgeat (almond and orange flower water) syrup or almond essence into 300ml (10 fl oz) orange juice.

1 Add the white and dark rum and apricot brandy to a cocktail shaker half-full of cracked ice.

2 Add the well chilled orange and pineapple juices.

3 Shake together well for about 20 seconds, or until the outside of the cocktail shaker feels cold. Strain into a tumbler of ice.

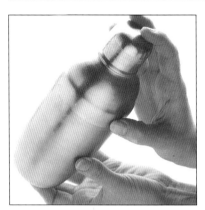

4 Slowly pour the grenadine into the glass and it will fall to the bottom of the drink to make a glowing red layer.

Morning Glory Fizz

A good early-morning drink, which should be consumed as soon as it is made, before it loses its flavour and bubbles.

Serves 1

INGREDIENTS
²/₃ measure/15 ml/1 tbsp brandy
¼ measure/5 ml/1 tsp orange
   curaçao
¼ measure/5 ml/1 tsp lemon
   juice
1 dash anisette
2 dashes angostura bitters
soda water, to taste
twist of lemon rind, to decorate

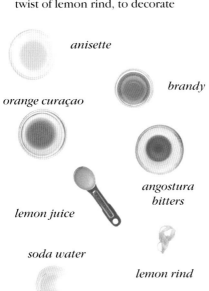

anisette

brandy

orange curaçao

angostura bitters

lemon juice

soda water

lemon rind

1 Pour the brandy, curaçao, lemon juice and anisette into a cocktail shaker containing ice and shake for 20 seconds.

2 Strain the drink into a small chilled cocktail glass.

VARIATION
Shake together an egg white, sugar syrup to taste, the juice of ¹/₂ lemon and ¹/₂ lime and gin or whisky instead of the brandy and add a splash of Chartreuse. Shake well and top up with soda.

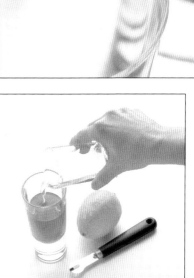

3 Add the angostura bitters to taste and top up with soda water.

4 Using a canelle knife cut a long thin piece of lemon rind. Curl the lemon rind into a tight coil and add to the drink.

Cider Cup

Cups make an excellent long and refreshing drink for
an apéritif or party. Mix up just before serving.

Serves 6

INGREDIENTS
rind of 1 lemon
slices of orange
5 measures/120 ml/4 fl oz pale
   sherry
3 measures/70 ml/4^{1}/$_{2}$ tbsp brandy
   or clove brandy
3 measures/70 ml/4^{1}/$_{2}$ tbsp white
   curaçao
2 measures/45 ml/3 tbsp amaretto
600 ml/20 fl oz good quality
   medium sweet cider
cucumber, to decorate

cucumber peel

amaretto

orange slices

lemon rind

medium sweet cider

pale sherry

white curaçao

brandy

1 Partly fill a jug with cracked ice
and add the lemon rind and orange
slices.

2 Add the sherry, brandy, curaçao and
amaretto to the ice and stir well to mix.

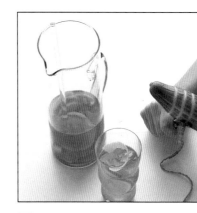

3 Pour in the cider and stir gently with
a long swizzle stick.

4 Using a canelle knife, peel the
cucumber around in a continuous piece,
to produce a spiral. Serve the cocktail in
chilled glasses, decorated with the fruit
and a twist of cucumber peel.

VARIATION
Instead of brandy, use Calvados for
a richer flavour and add a little
maraschino cherry juice to give
more colour.

Havana Cobbler

A very old-fashioned drink that is surprisingly refreshing served in hot weather.

Serves 1

INGREDIENTS
5 ml/1 tsp sugar syrup
1/2 measure/10 ml/2 tsp green
   ginger wine
1 measure/22.5 ml/1 1/2 tbsp
   Cuban or white rum
1 measure/22.5 ml/1 1/2 tbsp port

white rum

sugar syrup

ginger wine

port

1 Put the sugar syrup and ginger wine in a cocktail shaker, half-filled with ice. Add the white rum.

2 Shake together for 20 seconds.

VARIATION
Cobblers can be made with brandy, gin and sherry and even wine or champagne; for the latter, naturally, don't shake it and omit the port!

3 Strain the cocktail into a chilled short tumbler.

4 Tilt the glass and slowly pour the port down the side of the glass to form a layer floating on top of the cocktail.

Moscow Mule

One of the classic American vodka-based cocktails, which uses a large quantity of angostura bitters for its flavour and colour and enough vodka to give the drink a real kick.

Serves 1

INGREDIENTS
2 measures/45 ml/3 tbsp vodka
6 dashes angostura bitters
dash lime cordial
$^1/_2$ measure/10 ml/2 tsp lime juice
3 measures/70 ml/4$^1/_2$ tbsp
    ginger beer
slices of lime, to decorate

  angostura bitters

lime slices

 lime juice

 vodka

lime cordial

 ginger beer

1 Pour the vodka, bitters, lime cordial and lime juice into a bar glass of ice. Mix together well.

2 Strain into a tumbler containing a couple of ice cubes.

3 Top up the mixture, to taste, with ginger beer.

4 Add a few halved slices of lime to the cocktail before serving.

VARIATION

For a Malawi Shandy, mix ice-cold ginger beer with a dash of bitters and top up with soda water. Of course, the vodka does not have to be left out.

Vodka and Kumquat Lemonade

A mild-sounding name for a strong concoction of kumquat and peppercorn-flavoured vodka and white curaçao.

VARIATION

Use elderflower or fruit cordial, with gin or vodka as the base, and top up with soda or tonic water.

Serves 2

INGREDIENTS

75g/3 oz kumquats
5 measures/120 ml/4 fl oz vodka
3 black peppercorns, cracked (optional)
²/₃ measure/15 ml/1 tbsp white curaçao or orange syrup
²/₃ measure/15 ml/1 tbsp lemon juice
7 measures/150 ml/5 fl oz mineral or soda water
sprigs of mint, to decorate

white curaçao

kumquats

sprig of mint

lemon juice

black peppercorns

soda water

vodka

1 Slice the kumquats thickly and add to the vodka in an airtight jar with the cracked black peppercorns, if using. Leave aside for a couple of hours, overnight or up to a month.

2 Fill a jug with cracked ice and then add the curaçao or orange syrup, the lemon juice and the kumquat-flavoured vodka with the sliced kumquats.

3 Using a long swizzle stick, mix together well.

4 Add the mineral or soda water and a few fresh mint leaves and gently stir everything together.

5 Pour the drink (lemonade) into chilled glasses of ice.

6 Add slices of vodka-soaked kumquats to the glasses and decorate with more mint sprigs.

Horse's Fall

A long drink to serve on a hot summer's day. The addition of strongly-flavoured tea is a matter of taste and preference.

VARIATION
Substitute calvados or brandy for the flavoured tea for a Horse's Neck.

Serves 1

INGREDIENTS
1 lemon
dash angostura bitters
2 measures/45 ml/3 tbsp raspberry, Orange Pekoe or Assam tea, chilled (optional)
1 measure/22.5 ml/1½ tbsp clear, unsweetened apple juice
5 measures/120 ml/4 fl oz dry ginger ale or lemonade

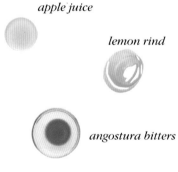

apple juice

lemon rind

angostura bitters

raspberry tea

dry ginger ale

1 Cut the peel from the lemon in one continuous strip and use to line and decorate a long cocktail glass. Chill the glass until required.

2 Add a dash of angostura bitters to the bottom of the glass.

3 Measure the tea, if using, into the cocktail shaker and add the apple juice.

4 Shake everything together for about 20 seconds.

5 Strain into the prepared, chilled cocktail glass.

6 Top up with chilled ginger ale or lemonade to taste.

Sunburst

Bursting with freshness and vitamins, this drink is a good early morning pick-me-up.

Serves 2

INGREDIENTS
1 green apple, cored and
    chopped
3 carrots, peeled and chopped
1 mango, peeled and stoned
7 measures/150 ml/5 fl oz freshly
    squeezed orange juice, chilled
6 strawberries, hulled
slice of orange, to decorate

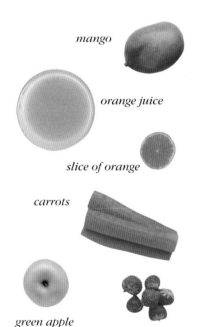

mango

orange juice

slice of orange

carrots

green apple

strawberries

1 Place the apple, carrots and mango in a blender or food processor and process to a pulp.

2 Add the orange juice and strawberries and process again.

3 If liked, strain well through a sieve, pressing out all the juice with the back of a wooden spoon. Discard any pulp left in the sieve.

4 Pour into tumblers filled with ice cubes and serve immediately, decorated with a slice of orange.

VARIATION

Any combination of fruit juice and yogurt can be shaken together. Try natural yogurt with apple, apricot and mango.

Scarlet Lady

This drink could fool a few on the first sip, with its fruity and fresh tones. It could easily pass as an alcoholic wine-based cocktail.

Serves 1

INGREDIENTS
115 g/4 oz Galia, honeydew or
    watermelon
5 small red grapes
3 measures/70 ml/4¹/₂ tbsp
    unsweetened red grape juice

TO DECORATE
red grapes, sugar-frosted
1 egg white, lightly beaten
15 g/¹/₂ oz caster sugar

red grape juice

egg white

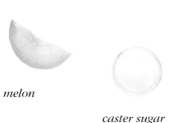

melon

caster sugar

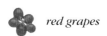

red grapes

1 Put the melon and grapes in a blender and process until they form a smooth purée.

2 Add the red grape juice and continue to process for another minute.

3 Strain the juice into a bar glass of ice and stir until chilled.

4 Pour into a chilled cocktail glass and decorate with sugar-frosted grapes threaded on to a cocktail stick.

VARIATION

For a longer fizzy drink, top up the melon and grape purée with equal quantities of grape juice and tonic or soda water.

Virgin Prairie Oyster

A superior pick-me-up and a variation on the Bloody and Virgin Mary. The tomato base can be drunk without the raw egg yolk, if it does not appeal to you. Use only fresh free-range eggs.

Serves 1

INGREDIENTS
175 ml/6 fl oz tomato juice
10 ml/2 tsp Worcestershire sauce
5–10 ml/1–2 tsp balsamic vinegar
1 egg yolk
cayenne pepper, to taste

balsamic vinegar

tomato juice

egg yolk

Worcestershire sauce

cayenne pepper

VARIATION

Shake together equal quantities of fresh grapefruit juice and tomato juice, with a dash of Worcestershire sauce. Strain into a tall and narrow highball glass.

1 Measure the tomato juice into a large bar glass and stir over plenty of ice, until well chilled.

2 Strain into a tall tumbler half-filled with ice cubes.

3 Add the Worcestershire sauce and balsamic vinegar, to taste, and use a swizzle stick to mix together.

4 Float the egg yolk on top and lightly dust with cayenne pepper.

Fruit and Ginger Ale

An old English mulled drink, served chilled over ice. Of course it can be made with ready-squeezed apple and orange juices, but roasting the fruit with cloves gives a much better flavour.

Serves 4–6

INGREDIENTS

1 cooking apple
1 orange, scrubbed
1 lemon, scrubbed
20 whole cloves
7.5 cm/3 in fresh root ginger, peeled
25 g/1 oz soft brown sugar
350 ml/12 fl oz bitter lemon or non-alcoholic wine
wedges of orange rind and whole cloves, to decorate

ginger

soft brown sugar

orange   bitter lemon

whole cloves

lemon

orange rind

cooking apple

1 Preheat the oven to 200°C/400°F/ Gas 6. Score the apple around the middle and stud the orange and lemon with the cloves. Bake them in the oven for 25 minutes until soft and completely cooked through.

2 Quarter the orange and lemon and pulp the apple, discarding the skin and the core. Finely grate the ginger. Place the fruit and ginger together in a bowl with the soft brown sugar.

3 Add 300 ml/10 fl oz boiling water. Using a spoon, squeeze the fruit to release more flavour. Cover and leave to cool for an hour or overnight.

4 Strain into a jug of cracked ice and use a spoon to press out all the juices from the fruit. Add the bitter lemon or non-alcoholic wine, to taste. Decorate with orange rind and cloves.

Blushing Piña Colada

This is good with or without the rum. Don't be tempted to put roughly crushed ice into the blender; it will not be as smooth and will ruin the blades. Make sure you crush it well first.

VARIATION

For classic Piña Colada use vanilla ice cream and 1 measure white rum. For a Passionate Encounter, blend 2 scoops passion fruit sorbet and 15 ml/1 tbsp coconut milk with a measure each of pineapple and apricot juice.

Serves 2

INGREDIENTS
1 banana, peeled and sliced
1 thick slice pineapple, peeled
3 measures/70 ml/4¹/₂ tbsp
   pineapple juice
1 scoop strawberry ice cream or
   sorbet
1 measure/22.5 ml/1¹/₂ tbsp
   coconut milk
30 ml/2 tbsp grenadine
wedges of pineapple and stemmed
   maraschino cherries, to decorate

coconut milk

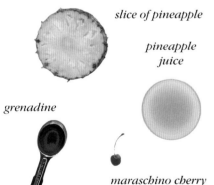
slice of pineapple

pineapple juice

grenadine

maraschino cherry

strawberry ice cream

banana

1 Roughly chop the banana. Cut two small wedges from the pineapple for decoration and reserve. Cut up the remainder of the pineapple and add to the blender with the banana.

2 Add the pineapple juice to the blender and process until the mixture is a smooth purée.

3 Add the strawberry ice cream or sorbet with the coconut milk and a small scoop of finely crushed ice, and process until smooth.

4 Pour into two large, well-chilled cocktail glasses.

5 Pour the grenadine syrup slowly on top of the Piña Colada; it will filter through the drink in a dappled effect.

6 Decorate each glass with a wedge of pineapple and a stemmed cherry and serve with drinking straws.

Volunteer

This is an ideal pick-me-up or non-alcoholic drink for the chosen driver at a party. It was devised and drunk during a very rough channel crossing in too small a boat!

Serves 1

INGREDIENTS
2 measures/45 ml/3 tbsp lime
   cordial
2–3 dashes angostura bitters
7 measures/150 ml/5 fl oz chilled
   tonic water
frozen slices of lime, to decorate
decorative ice cubes, to serve

tonic water

angostura bitters

lime cordial

frozen slices of lime

1 Place the lime cordial at the bottom of the glass and shake in the angostura bitters, according to taste.

2 Add a few decorative ice cubes to the glass, if liked.

3 Top up with tonic water and add the frozen lime slices.

VARIATION
Use fresh lime or grapefruit juice and a splash of sugar syrup instead of the lime cordial, and top up with ginger ale.

Steel Works

A thirst quenching drink, which is ideal to serve at any time of the day or night.

Serves 1

INGREDIENTS
2 measures/45 ml/3 tbsp passion-
    fruit cordial
dash angostura bitters
3 measures/70 ml/4¹/₂ tbsp soda
    water, chilled
3 measures/70 ml/4¹/₂ tbsp
    lemonade, chilled
1 passion fruit, (optional)

lemonade

passion-fruit
cordial

passion fruit

soda water

angostura bitters

1 Pour the passion-fruit cordial straight into a long tumbler. Add the angostura bitters to the glass and then add some ice cubes.

2 Top up the drink with the chilled soda water and lemonade and stir briefly together.

3 Cut the passion fruit in half, if using; scoop the seeds and flesh from the fruit and add to the drink. Stir the drink gently before serving.

VARIATION

For a Rock Shandy, pour equal quantities of lemonade and soda on to bitters or use your favourite variety of the naturally flavoured and unsweetened fruit cordials.

Bandrek

A rich and creamy version of the spicy Indonesian drink. Serve warm or chilled. If you like, add a very fresh egg to the syrup and milks in the blender and you'll have an egg-nog.

VARIATION

Stir ¹/₂ measure/10 ml/2 tsp whisky into the finished drink or add the strained spiced syrup to double-strength black coffee. Process in a blender with a little double cream, strain and serve over ice.

Serves 1

INGREDIENTS
3 whole cloves
3 juniper berries, bruised
cinnamon stick
6 green cardamom pods, bruised
4 whole black peppercorns
1 sugar cube
175 ml/6 fl oz water
2 measures/45 ml/3 tbsp coconut milk
3 measures/70 ml/4¹/₂ tbsp whole milk
cinnamon sticks and a maraschino cherry, to decorate

coconut milk

juniper

cardamom

cinnamon

milk

maraschino cherry

sugar cube

1 Put the cloves, juniper berries, cinnamon, cardamom pods and peppercorns, with the sugar cube, in a saucepan. Heat gently to release the aroma and flavours of the spices.

2 Add the 175 ml/6 fl oz water and bring to the boil.

3 Continue to boil for 10 minutes or until reduced to 30–45 ml/2–3 tbsp of spicy flavoured syrup. Remove from the heat and cool.

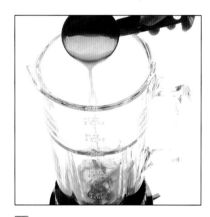

4 Pour the syrup into a blender with the coconut milk and whole milk and process until smooth.

5 Strain over cracked ice into a stemmed glass.

6 Decorate with cinnamon sticks and a maraschino cherry.

St Clements

Oranges and lemons create a simple but thirst-quenching drink which confirms that freshly-squeezed fruit has a superior flavour to any other kind that can be bought.

VARIATION

This same principle can be used to make pineapple, peach, grape and soft fruit juices, but sweeten with sugar syrup. These will keep in the fridge for 2–3 days.

Serves 1

INGREDIENTS
rind and juice of 2 oranges
rind and juice of 1 lemon
15g/^{1}/$_2$ oz caster sugar, or to taste
75 ml/5 tbsp water
slices of orange and lemon, to
    decorate

oranges

caster sugar

lemon

*orange and
lemon slices*

1 Wash the oranges and lemons and then thinly pare off the rind from the fruit with a sharp knife, leaving the white pith behind. Remove the pith from the fruit and discard it.

2 Put the orange and lemon rind in a saucepan, with the sugar and water. Heat gently over a low heat and stir gently until the sugar has dissolved.

3 Remove the pan from the heat and press the orange and lemon rind against the sides of the pan to release all their oils. Cover the pan and cool. Remove and discard the rind.

4 Purée the oranges and lemon and sweeten the fruit pulp by adding the cooled citrus syrup over the fruit pulp. Leave aside for 2–3 hours for the flavours to infuse.

5 Sieve the fruit pulp, pressing the solids in the sieve to extract as much of the juice as possible.

6 Pour into a tall glass filled with finely crushed ice and decorate with a slice of orange and lemon.

Dickson's Bloody Mary

This recipe has plenty of character, with the horseradish, sherry and Tabasco. The true Bloody Mary is a simpler version.

VARIATION
Use tequila in the place of the vodka for a Bloody Maria and use a clam juice and tomato juice mixture for a Bloody Muddle.

Serves 1

INGREDIENTS

2 measures/45 ml/3 tbsp vodka or
   chilli-flavoured vodka
1 measure/22.5 ml/1¹/₂ tbsp
   fino sherry
7 measures/150 ml/5 fl oz
   tomato juice
1 measure/22.5 ml/1¹/₂ tbsp
   lemon juice
10–15 ml/2–3 tsp Worcestershire
   sauce
2–3 dashes Tabasco sauce
2.5 ml/¹/₂ tsp creamed horseradish
   relish
5 ml/1 tsp celery salt
salt and ground black pepper
celery stick, stuffed green olives,
   cherry tomato, to decorate

celery
vodka
celery salt
tomato juice
fino sherry
lemon juice
salt and pepper
Tabasco sauce
Worcestershire sauce
creamed horseradish relish

1 Fill a bar glass or jug with cracked ice and add the vodka, sherry and tomato juice. Stir well.

2 Add the lemon juice, Worcestershire and Tabasco sauces and the horseradish, according to taste.

3 Add the celery salt, salt and pepper and stir until the glass has frosted and the Bloody Mary is chilled.

4 Strain into a long tumbler, half-filled with a couple of ice cubes.

5 Add a decorative stick of celery as a swizzle stick.

6 Finish off the cocktail by threading a cocktail stick with olives and a cherry tomato, and add to the rim of the glass.

Apricot Bellini

This is a version of the famous apéritif served at Harry's Bar in Venice. Instead of the usual peaches and peach brandy, apricot nectar and apricot brandy make this a tempting variation.

VARIATION
Instead of apricots and apricot brandy, use fresh raspberries and raspberry-infused gin or syrup.

Serves 6–8

INGREDIENTS
3 apricots
10 ml/2 tsp lemon juice
10 ml/2 tsp sugar syrup
2 measures/45 ml/3 tbsp apricot brandy or peach schnapps
1 bottle *brut* champagne or dry sparkling wine, chilled

lemon juice

apricots

sparkling wine

apricot brandy

sugar syrup

1 Plunge the apricots into boiling water for 2 minutes, to loosen the skins.

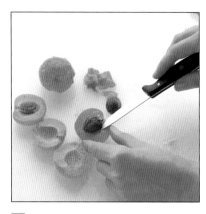

2 Peel off the skins of the apricots, remove the stones and discard both.

3 Process the apricot flesh with the lemon juice until you have a smooth purée. Sweeten to taste with sugar syrup, then sieve.

4 Add the brandy or peach schnapps to the apricot nectar and mix together.

5 Divide the apricot nectar between the chilled champagne flutes.

6 Top up the glasses with chilled champagne or sparkling wine.

Kir Lethale

The raisins for this cocktail can be soaked overnight in vodka.

Serves 6

INGREDIENTS
6 vodka-soaked raisins
30 ml/2 tbsp vodka or
  raisin vodka
3 measures/70 ml/4¹/₂ tbsp
  crème de cassis
1 bottle *brut* champagne or dry
  sparkling wine, chilled

crème de cassis

vodka-soaked raisins

champagne

VARIATION

For Kir Framboise, use crème de framboise or raspberry syrup and raspberry-flavoured vodka.

1 Place a vodka-soaked raisin at the bottom of each glass.

2 Add a teaspoon of vodka or the vodka from the steeped raisins, if using, to each glass.

3 Divide the crème de cassis equally between the glasses.

4 Only when ready to serve, top up each glass with the champagne or dry sparkling wine.

Brandy Blazer

A warming after-dinner tipple, ideal served with fresh vanilla ice cream or caramelized oranges.

Serves 1

INGREDIENTS
$^1/_2$ orange
1 lemon
2 measures/45 ml/3 tbsp cognac
1 sugar cube
$^1/_2$ measure/10 ml/2 tsp Kahlúa
pieces of orange rind, threaded
    on to a cocktail stick, to decorate

lemon

*orange rind
decoration*

Kahlúa

orange

cognac

sugar cube

VARIATION

Pour the hot cognac and Kahlúa mix on to freshly brewed coffee and serve black.

1 Thinly pare the rind from the orange and lemon, removing and discarding as much of the white pith as possible.

2 Put the cognac, sugar cube, lemon and orange rind in a small pan.

3 Heat gently, then remove from the heat, light a match and pass the flame close to the surface of the liquid. The alcohol will burn with a low, blue flame for about a minute. Blow out the flame.

4 Add the Kahlúa to the pan and strain into a heat resistant liqueur glass and decorate with the cocktail stick threaded with orange rind. Serve warm.

Long Island Iced Tea

A long, potent drink that has an intoxicating effect, which is well disguised by the cola. For a simpler version, use equal quantities of rum, Cointreau, tequila and lemon juice and top up with cola.

Serves 1

INGREDIENTS
$^1/_2$ measure/10 ml/2 tsp white rum
$^1/_2$ measure/10 ml/2 tsp vodka
$^1/_2$ measure/10 ml/2 tsp gin
$^1/_2$ measure/10 ml/2 tsp Grand
Marnier or Cointreau
1 measure/22.5 ml/1$^1/_2$ tbsp cold
Earl Grey tea
juice $^1/_2$ lemon
cola, chilled, to taste
slices of lemon and a large sprig
of mint, to decorate

 gin

Grand Marnier

  Earl Grey tea

white rum

vodka

lemon juice

 cola

lemon slices

 *mint*

1 Fill a bar glass with cracked ice and add the rum, vodka, gin and Grand Marnier or Cointreau.

2 Add the cold Earl Grey tea to the spirits in the bar glass.

3 Stir well for 30 seconds to chill the spirits and the tea.

4 Add the lemon juice, to taste.

5 Strain into a highball tumbler filled with ice cubes and lemon slices.

6 Add the chilled cola, according to taste, and add a sprig of fresh mint to use as a swizzle stick.

Mint Julep

One of the oldest cocktails, this originated in the southern States of America. Add fresh mint leaves according to taste.

VARIATION

Add a dash of chilled soda for a refreshing long drink.

Serves 1

INGREDIENTS
15 ml/1 tbsp caster sugar
8–10 fresh mint leaves
15 ml/1 tbsp hot water
2 measures/45 ml/3 tbsp bourbon
   or whisky

hot water

mint leaves

caster sugar

bourbon

1 Place the sugar in a pestle and mortar, or in a bar glass with a muddler. Tear the mint leaves into small pieces and add to the sugar.

2 Bruise the mint leaves to release their flavour and colour.

3 Add the hot water to the mint leaves and grind well together.

4 Spoon into a snifter glass or brandy balloon and half fill with crushed ice.

5 Add the bourbon or whisky to the snifter glass.

6 Stir until the outside of the glass has frosted. Allow to stand for a couple of minutes, to let the ice melt slightly and dilute the drink. Serve with straws, if liked.

Frozen Strawberry Daiquiri

A version of the Cuban original, which was made only with local Cuban rum, lime juice and sugar. When out of season, use drained, canned strawberries instead.

VARIATION
Substitute 50 ml/2 fl oz cream for the rum and brandy. Process together in the blender and serve as a non-alcoholic daiquiri.

Serves 1

INGREDIENTS
4 whole strawberries
10 ml/2 tsp lime juice
1 measure/22.5 ml/1½ tbsp brandy
   or strawberry brandy
1 measure/22.5 ml/1½ tbsp
   white rum
dash of grenadine
strawberry and a sprig of mint, to
   decorate

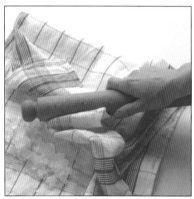

strawberries

lime juice

white rum

brandy

grenadine

*sprig of
mint*

1 Place ice cubes in a clean, folded tea towel and crush to a fine snow, using a rolling pin or hammer.

2 Place the strawberries with the lime juice and brandy in a blender and process to a purée.

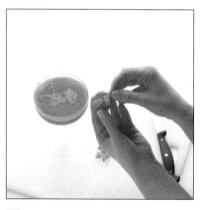

3 Add the white rum, grenadine and half a glass of finely crushed ice to the blender and process once more, to a smooth slush.

4 Pour the mixture into a well-chilled cocktail glass.

5 To decorate, remove the hull from the strawberry and replace with a small sprig of fresh mint.

6 Make a cut in the side of the strawberry and attach to the rim of the glass. Serve with a short straw, if liked.

Wilga Hill Boomerang

This sundowner is mixed in a large bar glass half-full of ice cubes, and is served super cold.

Serves 1

INGREDIENTS
1 measure/22.5 ml/1½ tbsp gin
¼ measure/5 ml/1 tsp dry
   vermouth
¼ measure/5 ml/1 tsp sweet
   vermouth
1 measure/22.5 ml/1½ tbsp clear
   apple juice
dash angostura bitters
2 dashes maraschino cherry juice
strip of orange rind and a
   maraschino cherry, to decorate

orange rind

clear apple juice

dry vermouth

*angostura
bitters*

*maraschino cherry
and juice*

gin

sweet vermouth

VARIATION
Drop the apple juice and serve over
the rocks or, if liked, substitute
bourbon or Southern Comfort for
the gin.

1 Pour the gin, dry and sweet
vermouths and apple juice into a bar
glass half filled with ice, and stir until the
outside of the glass has frosted.

2 Add the angostura bitters and
maraschino juice to the bottom of a
cocktail glass and add ice cubes.

3 Strain the gin and vermouths into
a shorts tumbler.

4 Add the strip of orange rind and a
maraschino cherry and serve.

Golden Start

A delicious and very drinkable mix of Galliano, orange, pineapple and coconut cream.

Serves 1

INGREDIENTS

2 measures/45 ml/3 tbsp Galliano
1 measure/22.5 ml/1¹/₂ tbsp
   orange juice, chilled
1 measure/22.5 ml/1¹/₂ tbsp
   pineapple juice, chilled
1 measure/22.5 ml/1¹/₂ tbsp
   white or orange curaçao
1 measure/22.5 ml/1¹/₂ tbsp
   coconut cream
30 ml/2 tbsp pineapple juice, to
   decorate
25 g/1 oz caster sugar, to
   decorate

Galliano

white curaçao

caster sugar

orange juice

pineapple juice

coconut cream

1 Put the Galliano, orange and pineapple juices and curaçao in a blender and process together.

2 Add the coconut cream with a tablespoon of fine ice snow and process until smooth and frothy.

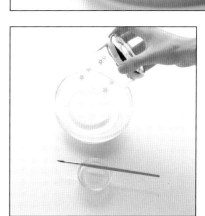

3 Rub the rim of the cocktail glass with pineapple juice and invert the glass into a saucer of sugar, to frost the rim.

4 Pour the cocktail into the prepared glass while still frothy.

VARIATION

Substitute light crème de cacao for the curaçao, to give that extra tropical twist.

Sea Dog

A long whisky drink with a citrus twist. For a sweeter drink, add a second sugar lump; if including Drambuie, only use one.

VARIATION

Use gin in place of the whisky and Pimms in place of the Benedictine.

Serves 1

INGREDIENTS
1–2 sugar cubes
2 dashes angostura bitters
2 orange wedges
2 lemon wedges
²/₃ measure/15 ml/1 tbsp whisky or
    Drambuie
1 measure/22.5 ml/1¹/₂ tbsp
    Benedictine
2 measures/45 ml/2 fl oz/3 tbsp
    soda water, chilled
maraschino cherry, to decorate

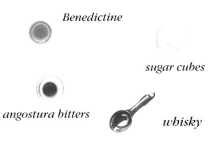

Benedictine

sugar cubes

angostura bitters

whisky

orange wedges

soda water

lemon wedges

maraschino cherry

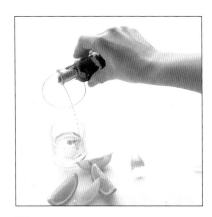

1 Put the sugar cube at the bottom of a Collins glass, add the bitters and allow to soak into the sugar cube.

2 Add the orange and lemon wedges and, using a muddler, press the juices from the fruit.

3 Fill the glass with cracked ice.

4 Add the whisky and the Benedictine and mix together well with a swizzle stick for 20 seconds.

5 Top up with chilled soda water.

6 Serve with the muddler, so that more juice can be pressed from the fruit, according to personal taste; decorate with a maraschino cherry.

Harvey Wallbanger

The next step on from a Screwdriver – add a dash of Galliano. Those who like a stronger version should add an extra measure of vodka.

VARIATION

Mix together the orange juice and vodka with a splash of ginger wine, pour into a glass and slowly pour the Galliano on top.

Serves 1

INGREDIENTS
1 measure/22.5 ml/1$\frac{1}{2}$ tbsp vodka
$\frac{2}{3}$ measure/15 ml/1 tbsp Galliano
7 measures/150 ml/5 fl oz
   orange juice
$\frac{1}{2}$ small orange, to decorate

orange juice

Galliano

orange

vodka

1 Pour the vodka, Galliano and orange juice into a bar glass of ice.

2 Mix the cocktail and ice for 30 seconds, to chill it well.

3 Using a canelle knife, take a series of strips of rind off the orange, running from the top to the bottom of the fruit.

4 Use a small sharp knife to cut the orange evenly and thinly into slices.

5 Cut the orange slices in half and wedge them between cracked ice in a highball glass.

6 Strain the chilled cocktail into the prepared glass.

Apple Sour

For those with concerns about eating raw egg, this variation on a Brandy Sour can be made without the egg white. Applejack or apple schnapps also work well, in place of the calvados.

Serves 1

INGREDIENTS
1 measure/22.5 ml/1½ tbsp calvados
⅔ measure/15 ml/1 tbsp lemon juice
5 ml/1 tsp caster sugar
dash angostura bitters
1 egg white
red and green apple slices and lemon juice, to decorate

egg white

lemon juice

caster sugar

angostura bitters

red and green apples

calvados

1 Put the calvados, lemon juice and caster sugar into a shaker of ice, with the angostura bitters and egg white.

2 Shake together for 30 seconds.

3 Strain the cocktail into a tumbler of cracked ice.

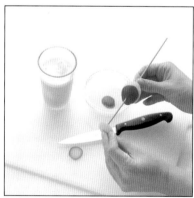

4 Dip the red and green apple slices in lemon juice. Decorate the cocktail with the apple slices threaded on to a bamboo skewer.

VARIATION

Sours can also be made with Amaretto or tequila; add a splash of raspberry syrup or port to the glass just before serving.

East India

This short and elegant drink can be served as an apéritif, dressed with a twist of lime rind and a maraschino cherry.

Serves 1

INGREDIENTS
²/₃ measure/15 ml/1 tbsp brandy
2 dashes white curaçao
2 dashes pineapple juice
2 dashes angostura bitters
1 lime and a maraschino cherry, to decorate

 maraschino cherry

 *lime*

 *angostura bitters*

 *white curaçao*

 brandy *pineapple juice*

VARIATION
Mix equal quantities of dry vermouth and dry sherry with angostura bitters and serve on the rocks.

I Put the brandy, curaçao, pineapple juice and bitters into a bar glass of ice.

2 Stir the cocktail well for about 20 seconds until chilled and strain into a squat tumbler over the rocks.

3 Using a canelle knife, remove a piece of rind from a lime.

4 Tightly twist into a coil, hold for a few seconds, and add to the drink with a maraschino cherry.

Planters Punch

This long refreshing old colonial drink originates from the sugar plantations found throughout the West Indies.

VARIATION
Add 1 measure/22.5 ml/1½ tbsp cold Assam tea, for a different tang.

Serves 1

INGREDIENTS
1 measure/22.5 ml/1½ tbsp
    lime juice
1 measure/22.5 ml/1½ tbsp orange
    juice (optional)
2 measures/45 ml/3 tbsp dark rum
10 ml/2 tsp grenadine
dash angostura bitters
soda water or lemonade, chilled
peach slices and a Cape
    gooseberry, to decorate

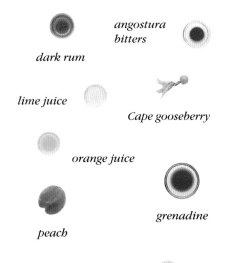

dark rum

angostura bitters

lime juice

Cape gooseberry

orange juice

peach

grenadine

soda water

1 Squeeze the lime and orange juices and add to a bar glass of ice.

2 Add the dark rum and the grenadine and mix together for about 20 seconds.

3 Add a dash of bitters to the bottom of a tumbler of decorative ice cubes.

4 Strain the rum and grenadine mixture into the chilled tumbler.

5 Top up with plenty of chilled soda water or lemonade.

6 Decorate with peach slices and a Cape gooseberry.

Singapore Sling

The origins of this old-fashioned thirst quencher lie far away to the east.

Serves 1

INGREDIENTS
2 measures/45 ml/3 tbsp gin
juice 1 lemon
5 ml/1 tsp caster sugar
soda water, chilled
$^2/_3$ measure/15 ml/1 tbsp Cointreau
$^2/_3$ measure/15 ml/1 tbsp cherry
    brandy
1 lemon, to decorate
black cherry, to decorate

black cherry

lemon

gin

Cointreau

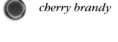
cherry brandy

caster sugar

soda water

1 Pour the gin into a bar glass of ice and mix with the lemon juice and sugar.

2 Strain the cocktail into a tumbler full of cracked ice.

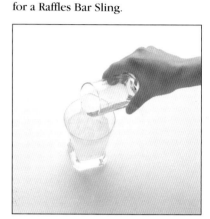

3 Top up the cocktail with chilled soda water, to taste.

4 Add the Cointreau and the cherry brandy, but do not stir.

5 To decorate, use a vegetable peeler or sharp knife to cut a long piece of rind round and round the lemon.

6 Arrange the lemon rind in the glass. Thread the cherry on to two cocktail sticks and add to the rim of the glass.

Kew Pimms

A very drinkable concoction of sweet vermouth, curaçao, vodka, gin and cherry brandy served over summer fruit.

VARIATION
Top up the spirit base with champagne, sparkling wine or tonic water.

Serves 1

INGREDIENTS
1 measure/22.5 ml/1¹/₂ tbsp sweet
    vermouth
1 measure/22.5 ml/1¹/₂ tbsp orange
    curaçao
²/₃ measure/15 ml/1 tbsp vodka
²/₃ measure/15 ml/1 tbsp gin
²/₃ measure/15 ml/1 tbsp cherry
    brandy
assorted soft summer fruits
1–2 dashes angostura bitters
2 measures/45 ml/3 tbsp American
    dry ginger ale, chilled
2 measures/45 ml/3 tbsp lemonade,
    chilled
1 lemon, to decorate
lemon balm or mint leaves,
    to decorate

lemon balm
lemon
vodka
orange curaçao
summer fruits
angostura bitters
sweet vermouth
gin
cherry brandy
lemonade
dry ginger ale

1 Measure the vermouth, curaçao, vodka, gin and cherry brandy into a bar glass of ice and stir well to chill.

2 Strain into a tall highball tumbler full of ice cubes and soft summer fruits.

3 Add the bitters and then pour in equal quantities of chilled ginger ale and lemonade to taste.

4 To make the lemon triangles, pare a thin piece of lemon rind from the lemon.

5 Cut the rind into a rectangle and cut a slit three-quarters of the way across the lemon rind. Turn the rectangle and repeat from the other side.

6 Twist to form a triangle, crossing the ends to secure. Add to the drink with lemon balm or mint leaves.

INDEX

INDEX